PLA

I looked again at Troy's lean, athletic build. I could just picture him in a North High uniform, and suddenly it hit me that I was sitting there talking to a gorgeous hunk from the football team. I, Megan Carter, who hadn't even gone to a school dance all last year.

"But," Troy went on, "I think that there's something else we could talk about now."

"What?" I had no idea what he was talking about.

Troy stared at the steps. "What I'm trying to say is—maybe we could go out sometime. We could see a movie or go to a party. There'll be lots of parties once football starts."

I tried to imagine walking into a party with this tall, incredibly good-looking guy. It was a fantasy come true.

Bantam Sweet Dreams Romances
Ask your bookseller for the books you have missed

Playing the Field

Eileen Hehl

BANTAM BOOKS
TORONTO • NEW YORK • LONDON • SYDNEY • AUCKLAND

RL 6, IL age 11 and up

PLAYING THE FIELD
A Bantam Book/July 1988

*Sweet Dreams and its associated logo are registered trademarks of
Bantam Books, Inc. Registered in U.S. Patent and Trademark
Office and elsewhere.*

Cover photo by Pat Hill.

ISBN 0-553-26864-3

Published simultaneously in the United States and Canada

*Bantam Books are published by Bantam Books, Inc. Its trademark,
consisting of the words "Bantam Books" and the portrayal of
a rooster, is Registered in U.S. Patent and Trademark Office
and in other countries. Marca Registrada. Bantam Books, Inc.,
666 Fifth Avenue, New York, New York 10103.*

Printed and bound in Great Britain by
Cox & Wyman Ltd., Reading

Playing the Field

Chapter One

"How many of those things do you plan to cook?" I asked my uncle as he flipped what must have been his eighty-ninth hamburger of the day.

"Well, if the Carter clan didn't eat so much, I—"

"At a reunion?" I asked in mock horror. Every year, on the third Sunday in August, my uncle Tony holds a family reunion, and, except for one year when it rained like mad, they've always been barbecues. My uncle Tony, who's just about everybody's favorite relative, has a fantastic yard for picnics—a huge lawn, tables, a stone barbecue pit, and a volleyball net. He even puts up a big canvas tent in case of showers.

"Can I interest you in one of my super deluxe chili dogs?" my uncle asked.

"Not yet," I said. "I have to work up to your chili dogs, and we just got here."

"I can see that," he replied good-naturedly. "Who did you bring as your guest this year?"

We have a pretty big family. With the first cousins alone, we are about thirty people. But my uncle is the model host—not only is every relative this side of the Arctic Circle invited, but also every kid is supposed to bring along a friend.

"I wanted to bring Beth," I explained, "but she's still in Boston on vacation. She has an aunt there who owns a bookstore, and Beth likes to hang out in the shop." I didn't add that I've never really understood people who hang out in bookstores. I mean, buying a book takes five minutes at the most. But then again, Beth and I are what my mother calls "different types." We just happen to be best friends in spite of that.

"A bookworm, huh?" My uncle was now setting neat rows of hot dogs across the grill. "Sounds like your brother, Mike. Where is he, by the way?"

I nodded toward the game already in prog-

2

ress. "Trying to smash a volleyball across the net."

Uncle Tony raised an eyebrow in surprise. "I thought you were the one who liked sports, Megan."

"They're OK," I replied. Actually, it had been a long time since I was into sports.

My uncle shot me one of those I've-seen-this-before looks and said dramatically, "She gave up sports to break the boys' hearts."

"*What?*" I asked, not sure how to take his comment.

"I'm just teasing, Meg. You know, that's what happened to your mom when she was about your age. She gave up a very promising career as a basketball player, and—"

"And the NBA still hasn't recovered," I finished for him. My mother is all of five feet two inches tall.

"Exactly." He handed two chili dogs to my little cousin Kelly and then turned back to me. "So you're going to be a sophomore this year," he said. "And what is it that sophomores do?"

It was a question I'd been asking myself. I mean, I knew I'd go to classes and probably do a lot of the same stuff I did as a freshman, but I also had this feeling that sophomore year was going to be very different. I'd never mentioned it to anyone, but right then I said, "I don't

3

know what it'll be like, but I think it's going to be special. I've got this feeling that something big is going to happen to me."

"You mean—"

But I never found out what my uncle Tony was going to say because at that moment someone yelled, "Hey, Megan. This team needs help. Come on over and play!"

I looked toward the volleyball net. A tall boy I swear I'd never seen before was waving at me.

"Why don't you go and show them how to play?" my uncle prompted. "You don't want to stand around talking to an old guy like me all day."

"You're not an old guy," I told him. "But it might be a good idea to get a little exercise before I attempt to eat one of your famous hamburgers."

Wondering about the boy who had called out to me, I straightened my T-shirt and headed for the volleyball game.

"At last," said that unfamiliar voice as I walked toward the net, "somebody who knows how to play. Now maybe we'll get somewhere with this game."

I followed the voice with my eyes. I could see the boy more clearly. He was tall and good-looking, with straight, longish dark brown hair, and dark eyes that were fringed with thick

4

lashes. My heart did a little flip, just looking at him. He was standing next to my brother, Mike, but I didn't know him at all, and I couldn't imagine how he knew my name.

I couldn't stand the suspense any longer. "Do I know you?" I asked. "Are we related? Long-lost fourth cousins or something?"

He laughed, and so did Lucy and Jerry, two of my first cousins, who were standing nearby.

"Maybe Troy is a kissing cousin, Megan," Mike said teasingly as he served the ball squarely into the net.

"Troy?" I asked. "Troy who?" But we were interrupted by the yells of the other team.

"Let's go!" shouted my cousin Randy, who was playing on the other side. "You guys playing or wimping out?" For years Mike has been trying to prove that we're not really related to Randy.

We started to play, and I soon realized that I was on a team that was losing—badly. This was probably because everyone was laughing and fooling around and trying to figure out things like whether or not you could make the volley-ball go over the net if you hit it with your shoulder. The score was something like eight to nothing, and Randy was disgustingly happy.

"Hey, are we going to let them get away with this?" I finally asked.

"It looks that way," said Mike calmly.

"Then again," Troy said, "we could always try something original like hitting the ball back to them."

The ball sailed over our heads again, landing just inside the line.

Lucy poked me. "Look at those big bozos over there, Megan. Do you really expect us to play seriously against them?"

For some reason I looked up at Troy, and he was looking at me, smiling. "Yeah," I replied. "Let's try something original."

After that, Troy and I started to play seriously, getting the ball and setting it up for each other, and then smashing it over the net. This seemed to bring the rest of the team around, and except for Mike, everyone made a reasonable attempt to play. Before long we had evened up the score. By the end of the game, we were ahead by two points.

Randy turned six shades of red and insisted on another game. But I'll say one thing for our team: We knew when to quit. After helping ourselves to frosty cans of soda, a bunch of us flopped down on the grass to recuperate.

Troy whoever-he-was pushed in through the crowd of cousins and sat down next to me.

"I knew we'd win with you on the team," he said. He was wearing a North High Raiders T-shirt and cutoffs. I found myself staring at his very tan, muscular legs. He was definitely well-built. In fact, he looked as though he had spent the summer being a lifeguard or something.

Again, I tried to figure out how he knew me. His face was starting to look familiar, and yet I still couldn't place him.

"Well, you seem to know me, but I don't know how," I said bluntly. I've never believed in beating around the bush.

"You've probably forgotten me," he said. "But I remember you. We used to play hockey together at the Winchester ice-skating pond."

"That was in the fifth grade," I said in surprise. "You were one of those guys? But they were all total savages. I mean, all of you seemed to spend half the game trying to knock me around."

"Not all of us." He laughed. "Anyway, I never saw anyone knock you down. You were a fantastic player."

"I was?"

"Of course. What other girl could have lasted on the ice with us 'savages'?" His brown eyes were filled with amusement, and I knew that I liked him. Not only for his looks, but also because he was down-to-earth and funny.

"I know my brother called you Troy, but I'm

7

afraid I don't remember your last name," I said, feeling a little silly.

"Fennell. Troy Fennell. I used to live two streets away from you. Your brother and I were good friends, but then my family moved to the other side of town, and Mike and I lost touch for a while."

"Troy Fennell—" I studied his face, and the warmth in his brown eyes seemed to jog my memory. "Were you the one who helped me when I sprained my ankle on the ice?"

"That was me," he admitted.

"You wore a green ski jacket," I went on. "And you were so *nice!* You were the only one who never slammed into me on purpose."

"My mother told me always to be a gentleman," he said in a light tone.

"And you were," I told him. "You definitely were." I paused. "So," unsure of what to say, I finally asked, "do you go to North High now? I've never noticed you there."

He shrugged. "I'm there. Same year as Mike, a junior. In fact, we were in chem class together all last year. But it's such a big school, you probably never noticed me."

Why hadn't I? I wondered. Maybe because my freshman year had been so crazy, I'd barely had time for boys. I'd barely had time for *me.*

But that was one of the things that I was hoping would change this year.

"Well, it's great to meet you again," I blurted out, without thinking. Then I realized how completely awkward that sounded, and I know I blushed. "What I meant was, how do you happen to be at my uncle's barbecue?"

"I was invited by Jerry Stone. He's your cousin, I think?"

"One of them."

At that moment I wished I had inherited some of the family's good looks, like my little sister Jessica. She's only ten, but she's got gorgeous green eyes and long, thick blond hair. "She's going to be a beauty," our relatives always say.

No one has ever said that about me. I'm tall and thin, with hair so curly that I don't dare let it grow too long. Beth tells me I have a pretty smile, which always seems like one of those things you tell someone when you think she's really a loser. But Beth says that I have a special sort of prettiness, a red-cheeked, outdoorsy type.

"How do you know Jerry?" I asked. My cousin Jerry lived a good twenty miles away.

"Would you believe we went to the same summer camp when we were ten?" he answered with a laugh. "We got lost together on this crazy hike—neither one of us was very good at reading maps—and we've been friends ever since. He's been telling me about these reunions for years now, so we decided it was time I saw one for myself."

"New game starting up," called Randy. "Are you guys ready to lose this time?"

Troy rolled his eyes. "Do you want to play again?" he asked. "Or should we let Mike, Jerry, and Lucy hold them off on their own?"

"Well . . ."

He smiled, a dazzling, white smile. "I just thought maybe—we could take a walk, or something. I've never been in this area before, and I'd sort of like to see more of it. What do you say?"

I thought for a moment. Was he really set on seeing this part of town or was he really asking to be alone with me? After all, at the party we were surrounded by all the members of my family and all their guests.

"Sure," I said, but there was a little quiver in my voice. "A walk sounds great. Why not?"

Troy and I strolled down along streets shaded by tall oaks and maples. It was an older neighborhood than the one I lived in. The trees were so large that they formed a green arch across the street. I felt as though we were walking through a long, cool tunnel.

"Megan Carter," Troy said as though he couldn't believe we had met again. "Do you remember how mad you used to get when we called you Meegles?"

I winced. "You had to remind me, didn't you? I hated that name!"

Suddenly I had a clear picture of all of us, so bundled up in jackets, scarves, and mittens that we could barely move, and yet we flew across the ice. "I don't think I've ever been picked on so much," I admitted with a smile. Despite the teasing, I had loved playing hockey. In fact, now it almost seemed as though I had never had that much fun, before or since. "But the more they picked on me, the more I wanted to become a good hockey player."

"Well, you were good," Troy said simply. "You were a real natural. What sport do you play now?"

I blinked with surprise. "None. At least not yet."

"You ought to," he said. "I can't believe you're not on the field hockey team."

I shrugged. "I don't know anything about field hockey."

"Anyone who played ice hockey the way you did would be terrific on the field," he assured me. "You ought to think about going out for the team. In fact, tryouts start next week."

11

"How come you know so much about field hockey?" I asked.

"It starts when football practice starts," he said with a grin. "And I'm on the football team. Both teams are out there together—you know, drills, practice, and then finally the coaches pick their lineups."

Field hockey. I thought about it with a little shiver of excitement. North High had one of the best teams in the state. Was there any possibility that I could make the team?

"Why don't you try?" said Troy as if he could read my thoughts.

"Actually," I confided, "this is going to be my big year for trying things. Last year I couldn't go out for sports, or anything after school."

"Why not?"

We'd come to the end of Trevor Street, where there was a big old wooden house with a For Sale sign on an unkempt lawn. There were no curtains or shades; it was obviously empty. We sat down on the front steps.

"My dad went back to school for an advanced degree last year, and so my mother went from working part-time to full-time to help with the money. It was just for a year, but it was really hard on my mom, so I took care of my little sister and helped around the house a lot—"

"Baked bread from scratch and scrubbed the floors?" he asked, teasing me.

"Almost. Mike isn't exactly Mr. Domestic, and every time Jessica 'cooked' we ate peanut-butter-and-banana sandwiches."

Troy laughed. "That's one of my favorite meals, but I can see how you'd get tired of it. You should have taught Mike how to cook."

I sighed. "Mike was busy being the school's literary genius. You know, he's on the school paper."

"He's a good writer, one of the only ones worth reading in that whole paper."

"I know," I admitted. "Even *I* like reading his articles. I just wish he could do his writing *and*—oh, never mind. Look, this is all in the past, anyway. My mom's going back to part-time work in a week. What about you—still playing hockey?"

"Not in August," he replied deadpan.

I flushed. "That's right, you said you were on the football team."

He smiled his dazzling smile, and I stopped feeling so embarrassed. "I play wide receiver," he said. "And if I could, I'd play football four seasons a year."

I looked again at his lean, athletic build. I could just picture him in a North High uniform, and suddenly it hit me that I was sitting there talk-

13

ing to a gorgeous hunk from the football team. I, Megan Carter, who hadn't even gone to a school dance all last year.

"But," Troy went on, "I think that there's something else we could talk about now."

"What?" I had no idea what he was talking about.

Troy stared at the steps. "What I'm trying to say is—maybe we could go out sometime. We could see a movie or go to a party. There'll be lots of parties once football starts."

I tried to imagine walking into a party with this tall, incredibly good-looking guy. It was a fantasy come true.

"All right," I said and realized how dumb that sounded. "I mean, I'd really like to."

"Then will you go to a movie with me next Friday night, Meegles?"

"Meegles?" I almost choked.

"Are you going to let that bother you?" he asked, grinning.

"I—" It *did* bother me, until I looked up into his eyes and I heard myself saying, "Not any-more."

"Good." He stood up, held out his hand, and pulled me up from the steps. "Then I'll pick you up on Friday around seven-thirty. Come on, we'd better get back before your entire family comes searching for us."

On the way back, we talked mostly about Troy. He told me he had one older brother, who was in college. His dad worked in the restaurant-supply business, and his mom ran a small boutique in one of the local malls. He was pretty sure he wanted to be a doctor, which meant doing everything he could to win a scholarship to college. Considering the past record of North High's football teams, he'd probably have to try for an academic scholarship.

Before I knew it, we were back at Uncle Tony's. We were barely halfway up the drive when Jerry came running toward us.

"Hey, Fennell," he shouted, "we need you for a scrimmage—touch football!"

"I guess you'd better go," I said, not wanting to embarrass Troy in front of my cousin.

But he didn't seem to be bothered by Jerry at all. "I'll see you on Friday," he said, looking into my eyes. Then he reached out for my hand and held it in his for a moment. Sophomore year was definitely going to be different.

Chapter Two

"That was a lovely barbecue," my mother remarked on the drive home. "I didn't know you were so good at volleyball, Megan. You were the star of those last few games."

"She's always been a natural athlete." I could tell my father was getting revved up for one of his pride-in-your-children speeches. "She takes after me," he went on predictably. "Remember when she was just a baby? She could run circles around any kid in the neighborhood, even the boys."

"Please," I begged from the backseat where I sat between Mike and Jessica. "Let's not have any Megan-the-Toddler stories." Listening to my parents talk about what a tough little tomboy I was always makes me cringe.

"Now, how was it they used to describe you?" Mike asked smugly. "Oh, that's right—built like a tiny Sherman tank. Of course you've stretched out some since then."

"You know," I said, "for someone who considers himself such an intellectual—"

"Nothing could ever stop Megan," my mother cut in irrelevantly. "She always had me chasing after her, even when she was only a baby and wanted to go on the playground slide."

"Give me a break," I muttered.

"It's your own fault," Jessica said, "for being so good at sports."

"That's exactly the kind of logic I'd expect from a ten-year-old," I retorted.

"Well, Megan," Mike said grandly, "at least the volleyball game gave you a chance to get reacquainted with the handsome and athletic Troy Fennell."

"Very funny," I said. "And also true, as a matter of fact. Was he really a friend of yours years ago?"

"Oh, sure," Mike said. "He still is, actually. We worked together in chem lab last year."

"Would you say he's a nice boy?" my mother asked. Even though I'd introduced her to Troy, she was concerned because of our date on Friday.

"Absolutely," Mike assured her. "He's smart, and he loves sports, especially football. He plans to be a doctor, I think."

"Megan's got a boyfriend—" Jessie chanted in a silly singsong voice. "Megan's got a boyfriend—"

I sighed deeply. My family didn't know what it was like to be in the middle. Being teased by an older brother and a younger sister was the pits.

"Oh, Mom. You want to know what Troy said?" I said, mostly to distract Jessie.

"What, dear?" asked my mother.

But Mike spoke up first. "Let me guess. He said, 'I love you, Megan darling. I have worshiped you from afar. I have always wanted to be on your volleyball team—' "

"That's enough, Michael." My father could be stern when the teasing went too far.

I gave Mike what I hoped was a withering look. "Troy said that he remembered my playing ice hockey on Winchester Pond. He thinks I'd be good at field hockey."

My mother turned around in her seat to look at me with excitement. "What a marvelous idea, Megan! You've been saying you want to make a name for yourself at North High School—"

"What do you mean?" Jessie asked. "Megan *has* a name."

"This is something else, Jess," I said. "You

know how you can feel really good when you accomplish something special?"

"Sure. Like when I learned to play that song on the piano?"

"Right." I stared down at my hands. I was twisting them sort of nervously. "Well, I want to find some sort of a special activity just for me. Something that I can be really good at."

"You *were* pretty awesome at ice hockey," Mike admitted, very grudgingly. I was always a better skater than he was and usually got the best of him in those hockey games. "But of course," he went on, "in field hockey, you have to start out on the junior varsity team."

"I know," I said. "I'd really like to try out for the team. Would I be able to, Mom? They're having practice sessions at school all of next week, and—"

"I don't see why not," my mother said. "In fact, I hope you'll try out for many things, Megan. Sooner or later you'll find what you're really interested in."

"If she's anything like me, she's very athletic," my dad said with absolutely no modesty. "I was all-star on three teams in college—"

"We know, Dad, we *know*," all of us said at the same time, laughing. My father has been telling us those college sports stories since we were old enough to listen.

In spite of our laughter, however, I felt just a tiny bit of nagging worry. What if I was no good at field hockey? What if I didn't even make the team? It was scary.

"Well, I'm going to be a cheerleader some day," Jessie announced, smiling proudly. "Courtney is, too. Courtney says we can start learning when we're in eighth grade." Courtney was Jessie's best friend and the ultimate authority on everything.

·"That's nice, Jess," I said, smiling. There was no way I could picture myself as a cheerleader.

"You'll find your niche, Megan," my mother said firmly. "Don't you worry. And as soon as I go part-time again, there'll be a whole new world of freedom for you."

I thought about that as we drove home. As I told Troy, our family life had been quite strange for the past year.

We live in a nice little ranch-style house in the suburban town of Northcrest, Connecticut. Everything used to be great before my mother started working full-time. My mom was one of those rare women who loved being at home. She worked part-time from our den doing typing jobs and still managed a beautiful garden, a spotless home, and lots of time for the three of us.

But then my father began to realize that he needed an extra degree to help him advance to a management position in his company, the Bardley Corporation. His mechanical engineering degree just wasn't enough anymore, he told us. And trying to go to school at night would take much too long.

My mom had offered to work full-time for a year and let him take a leave of absence from his job so that he'd be able to attend grad school full-time. My mom wanted to go where she could make the most possible money, and that was right at Bardley, doing monotonous assembly-line work. The catch was that the workers in the Bardley mill had to work swing shifts. They rotated to a new shift each week, from days to evenings to midnights.

"This will be very hard," my father warned us. "Your mother will be working day and night, sometimes having to do double shifts. She'll be exhausted and grouchy and who knows what else."

It sounded horrendous, and sometimes it was. But I figured that if Mom could stand it, so could we. It would simply be up to the three of us to keep the house running smoothly.

I found out very early, however, that Mike didn't think it was important for the dishes to be washed or the rug vacuumed. He was too busy reading his way through the entire North-crest Public Library.

And Jessica? Well, she was only nine years old when it all started. To be honest, she was pretty good at dusting and taking her clothes out of the dryer, but that was about the limit of her talents. Jessica is basically spoiled rotten.

I knew that all this had a lot to do with birth order—who was born first, last, and in the middle. I had studied up on that subject quite a lot.

In my desk-drawer files I have a collection of newspaper and magazine articles written by psychologists, especially by my favorite, Dr. Jane Pembroke. Beth always laughs at me for this, but I don't care. Dr. Jane explains things that no one else does. For instance, she once wrote an article about birth order and the development of the personality. I practically memorized it.

Now, according to Dr. Jane, this is supposed to be Mike: "Are you a First Born? Then you are undoubtedly serious, a person who has had to strive to achieve. You're always expected to live up to your parents' high expectations. . . ."

Well, a lot of that is true. My brother was born first, and he does have a major talent—writing those scathing articles for the *Echo*, the school paper. I hadn't exactly noticed him trying to live up to anyone's expectations, but sometimes Mike is hard to figure out.

Then there's the baby of the family: "Last Born? You are torn between wanting to be a baby without responsibilities and wanting to grow up quickly to be like your siblings. . . ."

Jessica fit that description to a T. Even though she keeps borrowing my makeup, she loves being the baby of the family. Responsibility is not her strong suit, but we're probably all to blame. Even now I find myself letting her get away with things because she's the baby of the family.

And here's what Dr. Jane Pembroke has to say about me: "Middle Child? You are in between, so you have to try harder at everything in life. As a result, you will find that achieving comes easier to you in time. In many ways you're much more relaxed than the First Born. . . .

"You are often the peacemaker, because you have to mediate matters between your siblings. You are extremely outgoing, and you have a desperate need to seek friendships outside the family. . . ."

Everything she said was true, especially the part about seeking outside friendships. I've always done that, and luckily I've had plenty of friends. Beth has always been the closest, though.

As for the part about being the peacemaker, I don't think I ever set out to be one. It just turned out that way. The first month that my mother worked full-time, each of us cleaned up what we thought needed cleaning. Neither of my parents was too thrilled with the results, so for the second month we all wound up being grounded. After that I got very inspired about keeping things neat. The only problem was, I seemed to spend half my time trying to persuade Mike and Jessica to help.

"It's all in your mind, Megan," Mike would say. "I do plenty around the house, and so does Jessie."

"Yeah?" I'd answer, "then why don't you take the garbage out, Mister Helpful?"

Anyway, we managed to get through the year without any major troubles. And now the era of my mom working at Bardley was almost over.

"This is going to be *your* time now, Megan," my mother said the day she told me that she was quitting her job. "I happen to think that sophomore year is an important time in a girl's life."

"Do you really think so?" I asked.

I should explain that my mother is youngish and still has very clear memories about what it's like to be in high school. In fact, she always tells me about the good times she had at North High School when she went there.

"It was for me," she said. "I want you to enjoy the rest of your high school years. Go out for things. Make your mark."

Make my mark. The more I thought about it, the more I knew that was what I wanted to do.

I was going to be great at something.

No, not just great. Stupendous. Outrageous. Sensational!

Chapter Three

Sure enough, when I checked in the local newspaper that night after the barbecue, I saw the announcement for field hockey and other fall sports tryouts. Just as Troy had said, Monday was the day it all started. All I had to do, apparently, was show up and put my name on the coach's list.

I have to admit, I was really scared the next morning when it came time to leave for the tryouts. I leapt out of bed early, being careful not to wake up Jessie, but then I stood there sort of paralyzed, staring into our full-length mirror.

Does this girl look like an athlete? I wondered. Or does she look like someone who just wishes she could play hockey?

I twirled around for a minute and stared at my body. Just as I thought—skinny. Tall enough, I supposed. No muscles that I could see. No fantastic biceps or triceps, since I hadn't been getting much exercise that summer, except for swimming in a neighbor's pool now and then.

No, I didn't really look like an athlete. But maybe being good at sports came from the heart, I decided. If I was really, really determined to be a strong player, then maybe that would make the difference.

"So calm down, Megan," I told myself. "The worst that can happen is that you won't make the hockey team. So what? So then you'll find some other activity at North High. Theater. Art. Chorus, maybe."

That actually relaxed me. It's one of Dr. Jane's tricks—talk to yourself out loud to calm down. I think it's got something to do with the sound of your own voice being reassuring. Anyway, I'd calmed down enough to start dressing.

I heard the front door open as I was tying my sneakers. I ran out to greet my mother. She had just staggered in after the midnight shift, looking sort of gray and worn out. I could tell she was exhausted.

"Well, only one more week to go, Megan," she

said. I could see her eyes light up at the thought. My mom is sort of pretty. Her brown hair still has no traces of gray, and she wears it almost shoulder length. She has nice blue eyes, sort of like mine but rounder.

I kissed her goodbye and took off for the tryouts. But she called me back and insisted on driving me to school. We live only ten blocks from North High, so I could have walked or taken my bike, but Mom said I'd need all my energy for hockey.

She drove carefully up the long, curved driveway that led to the school. In the distance, over a rise in the field, I could see the football field, with its bleachers and scoreboard. I knew Troy would be over there with the football players, and I wondered if I'd see him.

The high school itself sat on a flat plateau, its long, low buildings all spread out under the morning sun. The school looked as though it had been asleep most of the summer and was just now coming to life.

When we passed the hockey field, my heart started to hammer. Last fall I had sometimes watched the older girls practicing and playing there, never dreaming that someday I might be one of them. They had always looked so swift and sure of themselves, moving with precision, grace, and almost a second sense about where their teammates would be.

"I'm really terrified," I blurted out, my hand gripping the car window.

"Of course you are," my mother said gently. "We're always scared when we try something new."

"Not this scared," I said.

Mom laughed. "Are you kidding? You should know better than that just from all those columns you read, honey." She turned to face me for a second. "Don't you think I was scared when I first went to work at the factory?"

"I didn't know that," I said slowly.

"It was the scariest thing I'd ever done. I mean, I'm a terrific typist, but I didn't know anything about working on an assembly line. I was positive I'd end up in utter disgrace, with mountains of paper napkins piling up all around me because I wasn't fast enough!"

"You never told us that." I giggled. "Did that ever happen?"

She nodded sort of sheepishly. "Almost. There were times when I had some really awful piles on my table. But it was only because I was new, and after a while I learned. The point I'm trying to make is, every new challenge is an adventure. So you just get out there and go for it, Megan, no matter what the consequences."

"OK," I said, trying to sound enthusiastic.

Mom pulled up beside the entrance to the girls' locker room. "Do you know where you have to go?" she asked.

"I guess so. I've got to find the junior varsity coach, Mrs. Devine, and get my name on her tryout list."

"Then you're all set." She gave me a quick kiss and a hug. "Go knock 'em dead, kid!"

"Knock 'em dead," I repeated with a frightened catch in my voice. "Sure I will. That's exactly what I'll do."

The strange thing is, I almost *did* knock them dead, literally.

Before anything else, even before warm-ups or instructions, the coaches decided they wanted to see what we knew and what sort of shape we were in. So they put all of us out there for a trial game.

I turned into a lunatic on the field during that first game. The JV coach—chubby, middle-aged Mrs. Devine—started to yell at me and blow her whistle at me. She looked absolutely horrified.

"Megan! Megan Carter! What are you doing? Why did you slam into that girl like that?"

"It's called a check, I think," I said. "It's to

keep the one who has the puck from getting close to the goalie."

"Hold everything." Coach Devine dropped her whistle. "We're not playing with a puck here, Megan. This is field hockey."

"Oh, I forgot for a minute," I said, embarrassed.

Several of the freshman girls giggled. "That's called a ball, in case you didn't know it," one of them said.

"And there is no such thing as a check in field hockey," Coach Devine went on. "I don't know where you learned to play—"

"I played ice hockey with the boys," I admitted. "On the pond in my neighborhood."

Coach Devine frowned. "Your only experience was playing ice hockey?"

I nodded nervously. I was beginning to see that I'd made a mistake.

"Ice hockey is a very rough game," the coach said grimly.

"I know, but—" I stopped. I could see it wouldn't do any good to explain to Coach Devine how much I had loved it.

Coach Devine took a deep breath. "This is not a wild game, Megan," she said at last. "Field hockey and ice hockey have different rules. Now, I don't mean to sound tough, but you've got to get this straight, young lady. There will be no roughness in field hockey." She was staring at me. For the first time I noticed that she had big, bulgy eyes and small glasses that looked ridiculous on her face. She was wearing a North High sweat suit, just like the varsity coach, Ms. Mallen. But somehow Coach Mallen looked cool in hers. Even though she was very athletic, Coach Devine just looked dumpy.

"All right," I said, feeling embarrassed by the whole scene. "I'll remember that this is a different game."

"There will be no checks or anything else that you learned while playing on the ice. You will have to learn the rules of *this* game, or you won't last the week with us. Is that understood?"

"Yes," I said and realized I was angry. I began to suspect that the coach thought she could discourage me. Maybe she thought it might be easier to get rid of Megan Carter than to teach her the rules of this game.

Well, no way.

I was determined to play field hockey now, and to play it well. I'd show them what I could do. I'd blow them all out of the water!

I wasn't feeling so confident later, however, when I staggered out of the locker room at the end of the day. My muscles were all sore, stiffening up as though I were about ninety years old. It had been a long day of doing calisthenics, running laps, and practicing stickwork—how to handle the field hockey stick.

I was wondering what ever made me think I could try out for hockey. The idea of walking home seemed too painful to even consider. As I was standing there, wondering whether I ought to call my mom and ask her to pick me up, Troy came out of the boys' locker room. He looked almost as tired as I was.

He smiled at me. "So, how's it going, Megan?"

"Don't ask." I groaned and stretched a leg muscle. I thought maybe it would be a good idea if I never tried to move my leg again.

"What's wrong?" he asked, laughing. "A few sore muscles?"

"More than a few," I said. "And I don't think Coach Devine likes me."

"She's giving you trouble already?"

I grinned. "Every time I move I seem to be doing something illegal on the field. Did you know that they don't have checks in field hockey? And Coach Devine isn't too thrilled with my ice hockey background, either. She says I'm too rough."

Troy shook his head. "Maybe I should have suggested that you try out for football instead."

"Thanks a lot!"

"No," he said, "I didn't mean it that way. It's just that this year's team doesn't look aggressive enough. The new guys are about as spirited as that volleyball team we were on."

I laughed, imagining Mike playing football. "It's only the first day," I said. "Maybe they'll get better."

"Yeah, well—" He smiled. "Look, don't you let Coach Devine get you down. You're going to do just fine."

There was one of those awkward silences again as I noticed how good-looking Troy really was. He looked like a model from one of those jeans commercials. It was almost too much to believe that he might really like me.

"Where are you off to now?" he asked.

"Home." I had promised my mother that I'd get dinner ready.

"I'd offer you a ride," he said, "but my car's in the garage. New shocks."

"It figures. On the day I can barely move."

The dazzling smile was back. "Well, do you want to hobble home alone or can I walk you?"

"I'll have to think it over," I told him, straight-faced.

"You do that, Meg." He picked up my gym bag and started out the building.

"Wait a minute!" I grabbed for my bag, and he released it with a grin.

"Come here," he said softly. Then he put his arm around my shoulders and together we walked toward my house. I was beginning to believe that perhaps Troy Fennell liked me, after all.

"Let's have some order here, ladies!"

Coach Devine glared at us as we assembled for the second day of tryouts. She was standing by the edge of the field, surrounded by a huge pile of equipment.

"All right, now," she said, "we're going to have a review of positions and basics."

I soon realized she wasn't kidding when she said "basics." She began by holding up a hockey stick and explaining, "This is a hockey stick." When she went on to tell us which end was used to hit the ball and then held up a ball in case anyone was confused, my mind started to wander.

I found myself staring at the varsity players, especially the captain, Gina Bishop, and a blonde named Annemarie Martin. Both were seniors and looked tall, slim, and strong in their maroon-and-white shorts and matching varsity T-shirts.

Gina, Annemarie, and about four other seniors suddenly stood up, and I realized Coach Devine had called on them to demonstrate.

"First in the lineup are the forwards," she

explained, quickly arranging the girls into small offense and defense teams. "The forwards are offensive players who try to score goals. There are four forward positions: left wing, left inside, right wing, right inside."

As she named each position either Gina or Annemarie became the offensive player, smoothly maneuvering the ball through the defense. I couldn't take my eyes off them. In fact, I don't think I've ever concentrated so hard in my whole life. It was as if by staring at them hard enough my body would automatically absorb their grace and skill.

"Behind the two forwards are the two links," the coach went on. "Links have to be very fast runners, because they not only act as forwards and try to score goals, but they often run back to play defense as well." Effortlessly, Gina put on a burst of speed and showed us how one player could be both offense and defense.

By the time Coach Devine had run through the three halfbacks, the sweep, and the goal-keeper, I was in love with just about every position in field hockey. Everything except being the goalie, that is—that was one position that I knew was too tough. Besides, goalies have to wait for the play to come to them, and I knew I wanted to be one of the players bringing the ball down the field.

There was something else in Coach Devine's explanation that was beginning to get through to me: field hockey was *not* ice hockey. There weren't more rules, but they seemed stricter. A good field hockey player had to have terrific control.

Finally the lecture and demonstration were over and we were divided into teams for a scrimmage. By this point, I was aching to get out on the field.

Coach Mallen blew her whistle and the varsity players went to join her. Then we began to play. Nothing was more important to me than getting my hockey stick on the ball. But I wasn't very good at it. Learning to control the ball, whether for passing it, dribbling it, or driving it straight toward the goal, was much harder than it looked.

But partly because Coach Devine was still giving me dirty looks, and partly because I'm naturally stubborn, I played as if my life depended on it. I'm talking about one hundred percent. I zigzagged around people and stole the ball when I could, usually forgetting that it was against the rules.

Naturally the coach blew the whistle on me a lot. She'd call out the name of the foul I had committed.

"That was an obstruction, Megan." That meant

I had stepped between the ball and another player so that I was "hiding" the ball.

"Sticks, Megan." That meant my hockey stick was above my shoulders, a dangerous way to play. I was guilty of that one a lot. And there were times when I kicked the ball with my foot, too, and that wasn't allowed, either.

Oh, well, I was trying. If I didn't know what something meant, I'd ask and learn. I was determined to get this game down.

"You really are a terrific player," one of the girls said to me after a particularly hard scrimmage. She was tiny, with a round, dimpled face and blond hair, almost like a little Dutch girl. She was also fast and pretty good on the field. She was always there when I needed someone to pass to.

"Thanks," I said, brushing my bangs away from my forehead. "I think you're good, too."

"My name is Kelsey Kane," she said. "I'm new to this, too. I wish I had your talent."

"Right. Talk to Coach Devine about my talent," I said sarcastically. But I liked Kelsey. She was the first person on the team to act friendly, and that was important to me. It's part of my Middle Child personality, according to Dr. Jane Pembroke. "I've been noticing your game, Kelsey," I said. "You play a pretty good defense."

"Thanks. I know I'm not a whiz or anything, but I'd sure like to make junior varsity."

"You know what?" I said, suddenly feeling a whole lot better about the team. "We're going to make it, Kelsey. I have this feeling that we're going to make it!"

That second afternoon they had us doing all kinds of exhausting things like push-ups, more stretches, and running laps. By the fifth lap, I was ready to collapse. Kelsey was in even worse shape than I was; she looked as though she had never done much running.

"Hang in there," I told her with what little breath I had. "We'll get better at this. They can't cut us just because we're not up on our running."

The others, of course, the ones who had played hockey before, were seasoned runners. They'd been running a few miles every day all summer.

"That's all for today, girls," Coach Devine finally said, and there was a general groan of approval—and exhaustion—from the troops.

Coach Mallen gathered us together for a final word. Now *she* was a role model for the girls, a coach whom everyone looked up to. Ms. Mallen was a real athlete in her own right, having played varsity sports at the state university. She was a fantastic teacher and coach and was whipping the North High Raiders into shape. They were getting better and better every year. She usually wound up with division champs.

Coach Mallen was tall and long-legged. She had big dark eyes and a few freckles on her well-tanned face. She had a reputation for being tough, but everyone knew that she was a real softie if one of her girls needed help of any kind. I wished she could be my coach, instead of Mrs. Devine of JV.

"We're going to have a championship team this year," she told us in a simple but believable way. "Not only my varsity girls, but you junior varsity players as well. But you had all better realize that we have a rigorous schedule. When school starts, you all know that you'll be required to practice *every afternoon* after school, with no days off, ever.

"And this week's schedule will require you to be here every single day from eight in the morning until four in the afternoon. There will be no—absolutely no—excuses for not being here the full five days."

A girl named Mellie raised her hand. "Even if our parents want us to do something this week?" she asked. "Like go to the beach on Thursday with the whole family?"

Coach Mallen gave her a look that was cold enough to freeze a rock.

"If you go to the beach this week, you won't make this team, you can count on that."

Just then, out of the corner of my eye, I saw a line of guys lumbering past in a slow, steady jog. The football trainees. A hand was raised high, and I thought I recognized the runner as Troy.

I waved back happily.

Chapter Four

A couple of minutes later Troy managed to sneak away from the football team to come over and talk to me. I was just picking up an armload of balls, sticks, and shin guards to carry back to the locker room.

"Need a ride home, sport?" he asked, his brown eyes sparkling. He looked twice the size he had been at my uncle Tony's barbecue; I figured that was because he was wearing all that padding.

I suddenly felt great, having everyone on the hockey field see me with this good-looking football player. I'd never had a boyfriend before, just boys for friends. This was different. Troy and I had an actual date coming up.

"I'd love a ride," I said. "I think I'm even stiffer than I was yesterday—if that's possible."

"Can you wait another half hour?" Troy asked, continuing to jog in place. He looked faintly worried, as though his coach might come charging over the hill at any minute. "We don't get done for another twenty minutes or so. And then we take our showers—"

"No problem, I'll wait," I said happily. I was aware, suddenly, of the afternoon wind blowing through the maple tree on the edge of the field. From where we were, we could look down into the valley to see our town.

"Your hair is blowing into a million little curls," Troy said in an amused tone. His dark eyes were focused on me so intently that I felt uncomfortable for a moment. I knew I was crazy about Troy, but having him look at me like that—well, it was as though he could see inside me.

"I'll see you later," he said, breaking the moment and then sprinting back to his practice.

Kelsey came up beside me, also carrying a load of hockey equipment. "Cute guy," she said with a wink. "Is he somebody special?"

"Sort of," I said as I hoisted some equipment across my shoulder. "Troy is the one who suggested that I try out for the hockey team."

"He had the right idea," Kelsey said. "You

really are a natural out there. And you know what? I heard the coaches saying the same thing."

I swiveled my head to look at my new friend. "About me? Are you kidding?"

"Coach Devine said something like, if she could only tame you and make you play field hockey instead of ice hockey, you'd be quite an asset to the team."

I gasped in surprise. "What did Coach Mallen say to that?"

Kelsey laughed. "Are you ready for this? Coach Mallen said—'I don't know whether you ought to tame her. She's a dynamo just as she is. . . .' "

My heart stopped. "Oh, my gosh."

"Precisely," Kelsey said. "Oh, my gosh. They really are noticing you, Megan!"

Troy had a dilapidated old car that he called the Brown Monster. Nothing fancy. It was just an old Chevy with two weird gold stripes painted on it by some previous owner. But Troy was proud of it because he had bought it with money that he had earned the past summer.

"My parents told me I had to invest in a car," he explained. "I had to have transportation to my jobs, with all the crazy hours I was working, especially at Cinema Twelve."

"You worked at the cinema? I figured you

were a lifeguard, with that tan," I told him as we drove away from the school. I was stealing little looks at him. He was wearing faded old jeans and a Raiders sweatshirt, and he looked wonderful. His dark hair, still wet from his shower, smelled clean and somehow masculine.

"I was a lifeguard, too," he said. "I worked at the lake all day, and at the theater at night. I need to put away a lot of money for college."

"Two jobs—" I was really impressed. "Didn't you feel like you missed out on the whole summer?"

"No way. I had the best of both worlds." He was grinning as he shifted the old three-speed vehicle. "I had lots of sun, I could go swimming on my breaks if I wanted—being a lifeguard isn't exactly painful."

"And you got to see any movies you wanted, too," I said. "Pretty good deal. I wish I had known you sooner."

"Wouldn't have done any good," Troy said, turning to give me a quick look. "I had no time for dating. Not one spare minute, all summer long."

"Oh." I was secretly glad. That meant he wasn't involved with anyone, I reasoned. Maybe he had been too busy working to pay attention to all the girls who must have been crazy about him at the lake.

Still, I couldn't help being curious. Was there any special girl in his life right then? Or had there been someone in his past? I didn't have the nerve to ask.

"So—" Troy kept his eyes on the road. "How's the hockey going now?"

"Better, I think. Coach Devine still considers me dangerous, but I love playing. And you know what? I found out that even though Devine doesn't really trust me, she and Coach Mallen think I'm good!"

"I'd be willing to bet you're terrific," Troy said quietly.

"I don't know about that," I admitted. "But I'm trying. Now I want to make the team more than anything."

"I don't blame you," Troy said. "The field hockey team is one of the best teams at our school."

"How about the football team?" I asked.

"Not so great," he said wistfully. "And I don't know what it is. We have a good coach and lots of eager guys. We try hard, too, but—I don't know. They seem to grow bigger and tougher football players in all those other towns. Don't forget we have a date this Friday night," Troy said as he pulled into my driveway. "We'll go to a movie, OK?"

"Sounds great," I said. "If we both live through

this week of intense athletic training, that is." I was groaning from sore muscles again, and I felt my thigh muscles tightening up when I turned to open the car door.

"Wait a minute, I'll get that," Troy said quickly. He jumped out and ran around to open the door for me.

I looked up at him in surprise. "I didn't think boys did that anymore," I said teasingly.

"This boy does," Troy said with a grin.

All of a sudden, I felt confused and shy.

Troy reached out and ruffled my hair a little bit. "See you tomorrow," he said. "That is, if your muscles can wake up in the morning."

My muscles did wake up the next morning, but only just barely. I was sore and stiff all over and seriously considering staying in bed for the rest of the week. Still, half-asleep before seven A.M., my mind was already whirling with all the things I had been learning about field hockey. I took this as a sign that I ought to get up.

"A 'scoop' is a stroke that lifts the ball high into the air, sort of like using a shovel," I muttered to myself as I searched through my underwear drawer. "A 'corner hit' is taken by an offensive player when a defensive player unintentionally hits or kicks the ball over the end line. . . ."

Jessica groaned loudly. "I am going to knock *you* over the end line," she growled at me from under her blankets. "It's hardly even sunrise, Megan. Do you have to make so much noise?"

"Sorry, Jess," I said. "I can't help it. I'm trying to memorize everything all at once. A 'sixteen-yard hit' is—"

"Will you shut up!" she howled, upsetting our dog, Elmer Fudd, who was curled up at the bottom of her bed. Elmer is a small black beagle cross who likes his sleep, especially on summer mornings. He and Jessie made a good pair, in that respect.

"OK, pest, I'll get dressed in the bathroom," I said. "Will that make you happier?"

"Yes!" I could swear Elmer Fudd was saying it along with her. "And I suppose you're not going to make your bed again today, Miss Athlete of the Year?"

I stared hard at her. I'd been so excited about hockey and Troy that I hadn't even noticed I'd forgotten some of the basics around the house. I couldn't really believe my sister had noticed.

"Don't worry," I said, straightening the covers. "I'm doing it right now."

Chapter Five

The third day, getting out on the field felt as if I were going home. I wasn't at all nervous, as I had been in the beginning. And I didn't feel as though I was with complete strangers, either. I had learned just about everyone's name and even made a few friends.

I stood there in the right clothes—maroon shorts, a Raiders T-shirt, a pair of cleated shoes, my shin guards and holding a ridiculous plastic thing called a mouth guard ready to pop into my mouth whenever we played.

The adrenaline was surging through me, and I just couldn't wait to start driving the ball with my stick. But, of course, that wasn't the way we began.

No, first we had to do warm-ups and stretching exercises, standing in a circle, with Annemarie leading us. Then—guess what?—we had to run laps, sticks in position, for a whole mile. I didn't mind. I was getting used to running, but I was wildly impatient to get going with real hockey.

To be honest, I had Coach Mallen's words, as overheard by Kelsey, echoing in the back of my mind all the time. "I don't know whether you ought to tame her. She's a dynamo just as she is. . . ."

Oh, I wanted to be a dynamo! I wanted to show them all just how good I could be. So, the whole time we were fooling around with necessary stickwork or hone-your-skills exercises, I was picturing myself as Megan the Human Dynamo.

"Megan Carter, keep that stick down!" Coach Devine kept yelling at me during practice. "This is not baseball or ice hockey!"

Finally, we played a scrimmage game. They divided us into two teams, with each team having half JV girls and half varsity girls. That way the more skilled upperclassmen wouldn't outnumber us.

The two coaches assigned positions, and I saw them debating over where to put me.

"She can run," Coach Devine said. "Why not try her as a link?"

"All right, Megan, you try playing right link," I was told by Coach Mallen herself. I let out a deep breath. That scared me. I knew by then that link could be a vital position because there are only two links on a team, and they're right behind the forwards. Essentially, a link plays two positions, offense *and* defense, and at various times she ends up covering the entire field.

Scared or not, I went out and made myself look confident. I even slipped a headband over my forehead, varsity-style. Somehow it gave me a feeling of power. I gripped the terry-cloth cover of my stick, and I felt ready.

It was a perfect August day for hockey. The sky was bright blue with amazing puffy clouds that drifted above us, moving on the breeze. The field of well-tended grass glittered a vivid green, and the opposing team was in bright contrast to it with their maroon pinneys. I liked the way all the colors blended and blurred under the bright sunshine. I liked everything about hockey.

I wanted so much to make the team!

The whistle blew and the game started. I found out right away that a link does do a *lot* of running. I had to be wherever the action was, and that meant following the ball from one end of the field to the other. Luckily, I didn't get winded too easily.

In fact, I began to feel as though I were flying along on the wind. I was running, strong and easy, and I finally felt comfortable enough with the hockey stick so that I could charge in and maneuver the ball away from the opposition.

"Sorry, pal," I said a few times to varsity players on the other team as I scooped or flicked the ball away from them. Then I'd travel like crazy, taking the ball with me until there was a clear opportunity to pass it to a waiting forward.

The game was not going smoothly because most of us were either new or rusty and feeling our way along. But for me, it was almost like the old days in ice hockey; I didn't worry about the mistakes or the fouls we made. I just kept playing the best I could, trying harder each time.

"Megan Carter! Watch that stick!" I could hear Coach Devine shouting from the sidelines. "It's high enough to kill someone!"

Or, "Megan! You cannot thrust your backside toward that girl! It's absolutely illegal!"

Soon my team was making goals. That was the most exciting part of all, to see someone on my team send the ball streaking straight into the opposing goal cage. The goalkeeper was there, of course, but she didn't always move quickly enough to stop the ball. So my team began racking up points, screaming insanely each time we scored.

And then there came the moment when I had the ball and couldn't find anyone to pass it to. I looked up to see a couple of really big girls from the other side—one of them was Annemarie Martin—closing in on me.

I looked around frantically for a teammate to pass to, but there was no one. For a moment it looked hopeless.

The heck with this passing stuff, I decided, remembering the games on Winchester Pond. In those days I used to ignore the rules and go for it. Well, that's what I knew I had to do right then.

I was a link. I could try for a goal myself! So, full of energy, I charged out ferociously, hoping Annemarie wouldn't stop me.

But, no, she looked startled, and I took advantage of her confusion. I forged on past her with the ball. I made it to the circle around the goal cage and prepared to shoot.

I didn't have a lot of time to plan my shot, but I knew that wouldn't matter. Speed was the important thing. In my head, I was back on the pond, determined to show the boys that I could play hockey.

I took my shot. For a heart-stopping moment

it seemed as though everything was in slow motion as I watched the ball travel along toward the goal cage.

I could hear an intake of breath from the girls all around the field. The goalie actually fell over, trying to stop the ball, but she didn't succeed. The ball went straight into the goal cage.

"A goal!" shrieked Kelsey, running over to slap me on the back. "You made a goal, Megan!!"

"All rii—ight!" shouted Tammy Lowell.

Right then, I thought that was the most exciting moment of my whole summer. Maybe of my whole life. I had scored a goal against varsity girls—some of whom had been playing field hockey for years!

"Way to go!" shouted Gina. "That was terrific, uh—what's your name, again?"

"Megan." I couldn't stop smiling.

"Good work, Megan," Gina added, giving me a high slap with her right hand. *Gina Bishop*, I thought. The captain of the varsity team was congratulating me!

I was flushed and hot and high on adrenaline. I thought I couldn't possibly have felt any better than I did right then.

But then Annemarie spoke up. "What a show-off." Annemarie tossed her blond ponytail in a way that showed she wasn't happy to have been upstaged. She spoke in a clear, cold tone. "Megan

Carter must think she's God's gift to field hockey."

Her friends, seniors named Allison and Sue, looked at me as though I were some sort of dirt under their feet. "She certainly acts like a hotshot, for someone who just started playing," Sue told Allison in a whisper that was loud enough for me to hear.

I found myself blinking back tears. It just wasn't fair. All I'd done was make a goal. And weren't we all supposed to be there to give North High School a championship team?

Chapter Six

"Heard something good about our Meegles today," Mike said nonchalantly that night at dinner. Our family was seated around the dining room table, digging into a meal prepared by Jessica and Mike, no less—the two who had always claimed they couldn't cook.

With our mom sleeping days that week and me not at home to prepare dinner, Mike and Jessica had attempted a big potful of chili. It was definitely on the spicy side, but it wasn't bad. Well, not bad for beginners, that is.

My mother poked her fork at a mound of strange, lumpy hamburger covered with suspicious-looking chunks of tomato. "Hmmm. This is an interesting mixture, I must say. But what's this about Megan?"

Mike took a giant swig of milk before he went on. "I was at the library this afternoon, and I heard that my sister had scored a goal today in a scrimmage. Big-time stuff for a brand-new field hockey player."

"Is that so? A goal?" asked my mother. "Congratulations, Megan."

"I'm not at all surprised," my father said with a smile. "I knew all you needed was a little confidence."

"Are you turning into a jock?" Jessica asked.

Mike peered at me through his glasses, looking amused. "I suppose it's almost worth it," he said. "I'm referring, of course, to all the work that a certain someone doesn't do around here anymore, now that she's never at home—"

"Yeah," Jessie added. "And when Megan is home, she's always too tired to dry the dishes or make up her bed."

"By the way," Mike asked, "how do you all like the chili?"

Our parents were busy gulping down milk as though their mouths were on fire. Their eyes were wide with shock.

I didn't think it was all that hot, but then I've always loved spicy Mexican food.

"You two are going to be good cooks," Dad said in a strained voice, swallowing more milk. "You've made a good start, really."

"You might try putting in a little less chili powder next time," Mom suggested gently. "But, really, I'm proud of you both for making dinner." She turned to me. "And I'm proud of you for making that goal. I know how hard it is to do. I played field hockey for years, in high school and in college, and I don't remember ever making one."

"That's because you played defense, Mom," I reminded her. "But if you'd been a forward or a link you probably would have gone for it."

"Well, congratulations," my father said, raising his milk glass once again, this time in a toast. "To the new cooks in the family—and to our newest athlete. Long may they prosper!"

That week flew by, with each day busier than the one before. A few girls dropped out of hockey before the end of the week because the training was too rigorous. We ran, exercised, and played long and hard—most of us were turning into real hockey machines as the days went by.

The team lists would be posted by Friday afternoon. We'd know who had made the team and who had been cut. It would have been a tense afternoon except that we didn't have time to give it much thought.

It had been a week of scoring goals for me. Once I'd made the first, I was determined to do the same in every scrimmage. So I continued to pretend that I was playing ice hockey—but politely, in a less wild way—and I charged ahead to do my own thing. I racked up a good number of points for whichever team I was on.

It felt great, but I wasn't making any friends in the senior ranks. I was aware of that. Each time I scored a goal, there was a snide comment from Annemarie or one of her pals, Sue and Allison.

Sometimes I wondered what Dr. Jane Pembroke would advise if she were there.

After the final practice on Friday afternoon, Kelsey and I, along with everyone else, hurried through the girls' locker room toward Coach Mallen's office. The team lists would be posted by then, and our fingers were tightly crossed.

"I can't stand the suspense," Kelsey told me, but she started walking slowly as though she was afraid to find out the news.

"Come on, slowpoke," I said. "Look, everyone else is over there already—"

We stood at the edge of a crowd that was packed around the bulletin board. Some girls were screeching with joy. A few were crying, some just pulled away sadly and disappeared.

Might as well find out now.

"Come on, Kelsey," I said, pushing my way through the crowd. "Out of the way, you guys. Let somebody else take a look."

Kelsey was the first one to shriek. "There I am! I made it!" She pointed and picked out her name on the alphabetical junior varsity list.

A clammy feeling was coming over me.

I didn't see my name. I checked through the B's and went on through the C's and D's. And then I stopped.

They can't do this to me, I thought in horror. I had played so well all week! All those goals I had made, hadn't they counted for anything?

I couldn't stand it if they wouldn't let me play field hockey . . .

"Well, Megan?" asked Annemarie in a snobby sort of voice. "I suppose you've seen?"

I couldn't answer her. My eyes were filling with tears that I was determined not to shed.

"Don't you see, Megan?" asked Gina, giving me a friendly punch in the arm. "Look, you're on the varsity list!!"

The loud gulp I heard was coming from my own throat.

"Varsity? But that's impossible! I can't—"

"It's almost unheard of," Gina said. "But you made it. A new player and a sophomore— There's your name."

Kelsey gave me a wild, happy hug, almost knocking me over. "I'm so proud of you, Megan!"

"Don't think it's going to be easy, Little Miss Hotshot," Annemarie said, almost hissing at me. "When you get out there and have to play against varsity players, you'll be begging to get off the team."

I stared at her. I had never made an enemy before, and part of me couldn't believe this was happening. I remembered something Dr. Jane Pembroke had written: "There are times when you have to stand up for yourself." OK, Dr. Jane.

"I don't expect it to be easy, Annemarie," I countered, staring her straight in the eye. "But there's one thing I do expect."

"Oh, really?" Annemarie's voice was mocking.

"Yeah. When I get to be a senior someday, I expect that I'll have better manners than you."

With that, I turned and walked away.

"This calls for a big celebration," Troy said, whooping and picking me up off my feet and swinging me around and around. We were in the parking lot in front of the school, on the grassy area around the flagpole. Troy and some of the other football players had just emerged from their locker room, excited as we were because they had made their team, too.

"Put me down, Troy," I said, laughing. I was turning red because everyone was looking at us. "I can't take all this attention."

"Better get used to it," said one of Troy's

teammates, Dave Waldon. He was a real football player type, big, thick shouldered, and all muscle. He had light blond hair and a friendly smile. "You're headed for a powerful sports career, if you made Coach Mallen's team on the first try."

"We're talking celebration here," Troy said, finally putting me down and letting me un-dizzy my head. "How about one of our famous beach parties tonight, guys?"

At least eight members of the football team heard him and came over to where we were standing. "Party? Yeah." That was Joey Waldon, Dave's older brother, a fullback. "We can have it at our private beach. Somebody run and tell some of the girls. Never mind, I will." He took off toward a group from the field hockey team.

"But—I thought we were going to a movie," I said to Troy.

"Not on a momentous occasion like this. We've got to party tonight. Don't worry—things are always under control at the Waldons. Nothing rough. What do you say?"

I turned to Kelsey. "What about you, Kels?" I asked. "Will you go?"

"I'm not sure my parents will let me," she said uncertainly. Just then Dave Waldon clapped a big, beefy hand on her shoulder.

"No problem, Kelsey," he said with an amiable smile. "I'll come to your house and talk to your parents. I'm good at that."

She stared at him in confusion. "But—"

"No, really," he said gently. "I'm great at convincing parents that their daughter will be safe. Just let me try. You'll be surprised."

Both Kelsey and I started to giggle. Dave seemed so innocent and sincere that you couldn't doubt him. And we could see that he probably *was* terrific at winning over parents. He'd be polite and honest, and the parents would no doubt sense that he was trustworthy.

Dave was cute, too, and I could see that Kelsey really liked him.

I didn't think that I'd have any problem getting permission for the party, since my parents already knew Troy from the barbecue. So Kelsey and I both agreed, "OK. We'll be there."

"This is our primary kickoff party," Troy said, carrying a giant cooler filled with soft drinks from his car down to the beach behind the Waldons' house. "Everybody's in training, but we all deserve a night off."

I followed him down the steep path, carrying a bagful of frozen hamburgers. It was about seven o'clock that night, and everyone else was just arriving, too.

The path down to the beach went through a stand of hemlocks, winding around rock ledges and clumps of wild ferns. At the bottom, Lake Juniper gleamed dark blue in the setting sun.

"This is great," I said, looking around. The Waldons' property had a sandy beach that stretched out long and wide, with several picnic tables and a stone cooking grill. It was a good, hot night, but shade from the maple trees along the shore made it blessedly cool.

Kelsey came up to me, holding a giant bag of marshmallows.

"So your parents approved?" I asked.

"You wouldn't have believed it. Dave charmed them, just as he said he would." She blushed and smiled. "He's really a terrific guy, Megan."

"Mmm," was all I said, because others were coming down the path making an unbelievable noise. One of the guys had a huge cassette player blasting away on his shoulder. A familiar rock song filled the air, and everyone started singing along with it. By the time the song was over, we were all completely out of breath and laughing.

"Who's up for a swim?" Joey called, trying to put an end to it.

"Last one in is a nerd!" yelled Tammy Lowell. She was wearing a cute yellow bikini. Tammy forged ahead and splashed into the lake before anyone else could beat her.

"You field hockey girls are lunatics," Dave said, looking down at Kelsey with interest. "Are all of you that crazed?"

"Not all," Kelsey replied. "But when it comes to water, this one is!" She slipped out of her clothes, revealing an Olympic-style blue suit, and followed Tammy into the water.

Underneath my outfit was a new Hawaiian-print bathing suit that somehow managed to make even my body look curvy. In seconds I was gliding through the velvety water, with dark blue ripples all around me.

Pretty soon almost everyone was in the lake, except for Annemarie, who said she didn't want to get her hair wet. The water felt wonderfully warm with only an occasional cold patch. Swimming was like a reward for that whole grueling week of hard training.

"Hey, mermaid." Troy was suddenly swimming beside me, looking wonderful with his hair all wet and drops of water on his thick eyelashes.

I ran my palm through the water, splashing him, then dove under before he could get me back.

I felt a tug at my heels and then Troy surfaced beside me. "Do you want to swim out to the raft?" he asked.

"Sure."

We glided together toward the raft, which was about twenty yards out from the beach. It was quiet out there; almost everyone else had gone back for food.

The sun was dipping low in the west, casting deep red shadows across the trees and over the calm water. There was a hush in the air, with only the sound of some chirping birds and the night crickets. It was very peaceful.

Sighing with contentment, I raised my arms and grabbed onto the wooden planks of the raft. It felt good to rest and just let my legs dangle in the water.

Troy reached out with one forefinger and touched my nose. "Do you know you have a slightly turned-up nose?"

I shrugged. "It's the official Carter family nose."

"Well, it's much cuter on you than on your brother." His finger stayed there for a fraction of a second, and I was very aware of how warm his skin felt against mine. I was feeling all tingly, as though some sort of electricity was going through me.

"This party's great," I said. I looked back toward the shore, where fires were glowing and a volleyball game had been started. "I've never been to anything like this before."

"Now and then I get a good idea."

I poked at a splinter in the raft wood. I couldn't help wondering again about the girls Troy might have dated in the past. "So, who did you bring to your parties last year?" I asked casually.

Troy's brown eyes were fixed right on me.

The corners of his mouth turned up a little bit in amusement.

"Are you asking who my girlfriend used to be, Megan?"

I smiled with him. "I guess I am, yes."

His arm reached up beside mine to grab hold of the raft. I stared at his smooth, powerful muscles.

"Well, if you really want to know, her name was Leslie, and she moved away last June. Her family went to California."

"Oh. That's too bad," I lied.

"No." He moved a little closer to me, though he didn't touch me at all. "I'm glad now that she did move away," he said.

"That's a terrible thing to say."

"No, it's not. She met someone else out there, and I was lucky, too. I went to your uncle's barbecue. I'm glad I got the chance to meet up with you again, Megan."

Chapter Seven

Our fingers touched up there on the raft. It was a simple thing, but it was very special to me. Even now, I'm not sure why. I mean, we'd held hands before, and I'd even gotten used to the feel of his arm around me, but our hands touching like that seemed like some sort of bonding. We were friends, yet this made us more than friends.

We were side by side next to the raft, about as close together as two people can be. Troy was looking at me, and again I found I couldn't meet his eyes. I looked down at the surface of the lake and started to chatter like a fool.

"Look at all of them on the beach! They must

be eating up all those hamburgers and rolls. I wonder if they'll leave any for us?"

Troy took his cue from me, I suppose. I think he would have kissed me, out there in the water, if I hadn't been such a blink-brain. But since I was chattering, he eased his fingers away from mine, sighing just a little bit, and pushed back in the water.

"OK," he said. "Do you want to go back for some food?"

No, not really, I thought unexpectedly. I wanted Troy to kiss me, but I realized that too late. The moment had passed. Why was I so afraid to let him see how I felt?

We swam back together, at first in perfect synchronization. Then Troy pulled out in front of me.

"Come on, jock, can't you keep up?" he asked, teasing me.

For an answer, I caught up with him.

"I can even catch up with a wide receiver," I said.

"Yeah, from the pathetic football team of North High," he reminded me, "while you happen to be the first sophomore to make varsity in Coach Mallen's super-champion team." He wasn't speaking at all bitterly, though. He seemed glad for me and sort of proud, I thought, that he had encouraged me to try out for field hockey.

Still, I felt a bit uneasy about the situation. I wished that the football team would undergo some miraculous change.

"You've eaten enough!" Kelsey was scolding Dave almost like a mother. It really was ridiculous, considering that she was so tiny and he was as big as one of the Berkshire Mountains. They looked funny together, but there must have been chemistry between them because Dave was staying close by her side the whole evening, and he actually put down a triple cheeseburger.

Troy and I were staying close, too. We had our supper together, played some volleyball, and then sat down to relax.

The final rays of the sun were disappearing by then, so that the beach was shrouded in darkness except for the firelight. Everyone seemed to have drifted off into little groups or couples. Troy and I sat apart from the others under the maple tree. Again, I wished that he'd kiss me.

But Troy knew how to play it cool. His arm stayed around me, solid and possessive, but he seemed to be biding his time, waiting for a signal from me.

I felt another attack of shyness coming on. I don't know why they kept coming, but when they did, they were nearly paralyzing. I couldn't think of anything to say or do that wouldn't seem incredibly dumb. I'd never been in a situation like that before. And I knew this was not a moment for my psychology articles, either—sorry, Dr. Jane.

I studied Troy's face as he leaned back against the tree. Firelight flickered against his features, making him look even more gorgeous than usual. I wished I could memorize that evening for the rest of my life, so that whenever I wanted I would be able to imagine Troy sitting there beside me.

"Troy," I began, not knowing what I was about to do. I put out my hand and touched his cheek, just a feather-light touch that somehow felt so right.

It was the signal Troy had been waiting for. He pulled me closer to him until his mouth was near enough for me to feel his breath on my cheek.

It was a long, warm kiss, a kind of promise of what was to come. I loved the way his mouth felt against mine, and the way I felt, snuggled up close to his chest there on the beach.

"Hey, what's going on here?" demanded Dave, giving Troy a friendly *thunk* on the head. "Didn't you hear the new rules? No fraternizing with members of any other school team."

"Yeah, sure," Troy said, reaching around to try to smack his friend back. "That'll go for you and Kelsey, too, then."

"Oh," Dave said with his arm around Kelsey. They sat down in the sand beside us. "Forget that rule, then."

"Thanks, Waldon," Troy said.

I was only half listening to them. The rest of me was remembering Troy's kiss—my very first kiss.

I remembered how I had thought that making that first field hockey goal in scrimmage was the most wonderful moment of my life. Well, now I was ready to revise that.

That moment, right there on the beach with Troy, was now the all-time champion most wonderful moment of my life!

Chapter Eight

I was nearly turning cartwheels on Monday morning. It was the first day of school and the first day of the field hockey season!

"And the first day that Mom doesn't have to go to work at Bardley," Jessie reminded me. We were all gathered in the kitchen, dressed and ready for a new school year. Even Mike, trying to appear cool and unconcerned, was wearing a new rugby shirt. I had to admit he looked pretty good, even though he was my brother.

Jessica had dressed with care. I smiled, remembering when I was in grade school. I always wanted to wear something brand-new—just like the cotton skirt that Jessie was wearing with her new shoes and sweater.

But not this year. Kelsey and I had decided it'd be better if we wore something old and faded. I had found a faded pair of jeans, but my bright red oversized shirt was sort of new. I had bought it during a shopping trip with Beth last spring.

My mother smiled as she looked at all of us in our back-to-school outfits. She was standing at the stove, busily frying up bacon and eggs.

"So how does it feel to be retired?" I asked. "Just imagine, no more rotating shifts."

But my mother looked slightly worried. "I've been wondering about that. I guess I'll get the typing started again, but that'll still leave me with a lot of free time—"

"You were dying to be a homemaker again," Dad said, looking puzzled. "Are you getting cold feet now?"

Mom shook her head ruefully. "Isn't it silly? Yes, I guess I am, but it'll pass. It's just going to be strange for a while, not rushing off to punch a time clock somewhere."

"I think it's going to be terrific," Dad said. He had hated her working at the mill.

My mother flipped the bacon. "Maybe I'll become one of those compulsive shoppers," she mused out loud. "Buying new lingerie and shoes and changing the draperies every few weeks—"

"You?" Mike hooted. "You'd become an astronaut first."

"That's an idea," she said quietly, and it hit me with a pang that my mother had changed. Somehow, her old life wasn't going to be enough for her anymore.

"Well, at least I can get to some of Megan's hockey games," she finished, setting out a small glass of orange juice for each of us. The breakfast table looked amazingly pretty. There were flowered place mats and colorful paper napkins, and a small bouquet of mums as a centerpiece. Unreal. We were eating at a table that looked as if it belonged in *Better Homes and Gardens*. I thought back to the times before my mom had gone to work at the factory. Things had never been this fancy. I couldn't help thinking that Dr. Jane Pembroke would have said that this woman was overcompensating. I figured that meant that my mother was trying to prove something to herself. But what?

"Megan!" cried a familiar voice. It was Beth, running down the hall toward me.

"I just got back from Boston late last night," she began breathlessly. "The plane circled the airport for two hours. Landing took longer than the flight!"

"I'm so glad you're back," I told her. "I missed you so much!"

It had been a month since we'd seen each

other. Beth was slender with reddish-brown hair. She wore big glasses that made her look extremely serious and studious—until you got to know her. Now she looked taller and prettier than she had when she'd left for Boston. How much can a person change in a month? I wondered.

"Tell me what's happening," Beth said. "I feel as if I've been away forever!"

"Well, for starters—I made the field hockey team."

Sports have never been of much interest to Beth. She looked at me cynically. "You mean you really want to spend the entire fall listening to Devine scream at everyone? Yuck! Gym class if more than enough for me."

"It's not Devine," I said. "You're not going to believe this, Beth, but—I made varsity!"

She stared at me. "You're right, I can't believe that— Whew, varsity." Her blue eyes, behind the big red frames, looked concerned. "I mean, I'm glad for you, but—aren't you worried, Megan?"

"What do you mean?"

"About—about the pressure. All the experience those other girls have, compared with you." Her face turned red and she stopped. "Oh, I'm sorry, I don't mean to be so negative. I think it's terrific, I really do. I'm sure the coach put you on the team because she knows you can do it."

"I hope so," I said. But there was a little nagging feeling of doubt behind my words. To be honest, I was scared about playing on the varsity team. Secretly, I felt that I belonged in JV with the girls my own age.

"Coach Mallen is one pretty smart cookie, from what I hear," Beth said reassuringly.

"Yeah, but I'm sort of nervous," I admitted. "You hit the nail on the head when you said that about pressure."

"Oh, I'm sorry, Megan."

"No, no. I'm glad I'm admitting it to myself and you. After all, what is it that Dr. Jane says in all her articles? We must *admit* our feelings. Understand what we are experiencing—"

"Oh, you and your Dr. Jane," Beth groaned. "Look, I have an idea. Why don't you go and tell the coach how you feel?"

"Maybe I will," I said, "but—hey, what about you? Did you have fun in Boston?"

"I loved it. Almost didn't want to come back, except I am excited to be on the *Echo* staff. Meet the Brenda Starr of North High."

"That's right, I'd almost forgotten."

"How could you?" Beth asked with a laugh.

She had a point. Ever since I had known Beth, she has wanted to be a journalist. And she nearly drove everyone crazy last spring when she had to write a sample column to get onto the newspaper staff.

"Did you fall in love in Boston?" I asked, suddenly suspicious that that was why she was so happy there.

"I wish! Actually, I've got my eye on somebody here. Someone else who's on the paper."

"You're being awfully vague. Aren't you going to tell me his name?"

She blushed. "I can't just yet, so please don't ask."

"Why, for heaven's sake?" I was dying of curiosity.

"For a very good reason. Tell me about you, Megan."

Wondering who Beth's secret love was, I told her about Troy Fennell, including the Friday night beach party. "And then we went out Saturday to the movies with Kelsey—she's a new friend from hockey—and Dave Waldon—"

"It sounds like your time has really come."

"Huh?"

Beth spoke in a mock-motherly sort of tone. "My grandmother always said, everyone's time comes around sooner or later, if she's a good and hardworking person."

"Oh, that's a nice thought."

"Seriously, you've been working hard, taking care of Jessica and all that housework stuff while your mom worked." Beth made a victory sign. "Your time has come around, Megan."

As we separated to go to our classes, I was still wondering whom Beth had a crush on and why she wouldn't tell me. We had always told each other everything. Someone on the newspaper, she had said . . .

I almost bumped into the door to the woodworking shop. An odd idea had just crossed my mind. It was kind of crazy, but—could Beth's mysterious crush possibly be on my own brother?

I kept looking for Troy, but I never ran into him. North High is a really big school, and I knew I could go for days without seeing someone who's in another grade. I hoped that wouldn't happen. I really wanted to see him on the first day of school, just as a sort of symbol of the new feeling that was between us.

But in the meantime, I asked for a pass from my fourth-period study hall so I could talk to Coach Mallen. I wouldn't have done it if I hadn't been feeling so nervous. But it seemed important to talk with her, face to face.

I went down to her office, a tiny cubicle right next to the girls' locker room. I'd been told she didn't have a gym class that period, but she wasn't in her office when I got there.

For a few minutes I stood in the cramped office, not sure of what I should do. I stared at

Coach Mallen's desk, piled high with papers. Then I stared at the equipment lying helter-skelter all over the floor—hockey sticks and balls in boxes, crates of shin guards, and someone's old cleated shoes. I found myself drawn to the pictures on the walls. They were photographs of the championship field hockey teams from all the previous years. I stared at them and swallowed hard.

Dozens of faces looked out at me from those photos. Girls of all colors and sizes, with all sorts of hairstyles and makeup. But they all had one thing in common, and it scared me to death.

They all looked confident.

They all knew how to play field hockey—and play it well. And me? I was just a beginner. I was still trying to learn the rules. What was I doing on the best field hockey team in this whole section of the state?

I shivered involuntarily as I continued to stare at the glossy faces of North High's athletes.

"Did you want to see me, Megan?" Coach Mallen had entered the office without my hearing her. She wore sneakers, of course, and a maroon sweat suit. She looked tall and confident, as she always did, and she scared me every bit as much as the pictures on the wall had!

"Yes." I took a deep breath and said all in a jumble, "I'm feeling really scared. I don't know—I can't see how I can ever play varsity, when I'm so new at this game. I can't—I can't imagine getting out there against really skilled girls from other schools—"

The coach motioned for me to have a seat, and she sat down on her swivel chair behind the desk.

"First of all, calm down, Megan. I'm glad you came to me. It's no good keeping it all inside you."

"Well," I said, "I've been feeling two ways. First, excited and happy because I made the team, but second, just plain terrified because I've never played field hockey before."

"I know." She sat back and observed me. "Well, it is highly unusual to put a sophomore on varsity, Megan. And I wouldn't have done it if I'd had enough experienced girls for all the positions on my team."

She hastened to add, "Not that you aren't good enough. That's not true. You are. I just mean that I would have kept older girls there if I could, but as it turned out, many of last year's players left to get jobs, or to run Cross Country, or for various other reasons."

"I see."

"But I chose you, Megan, because you're a

powerful player. I really do believe you can handle whatever comes along, and I think you'll be an asset to the team."

"Thank you," I said. "But—"

"Yes?"

"Some of the girls have already called me a hotshot and a show-off, and told me that it won't be easy. I'm not trying to rat on anyone, I'm just telling you my problem in full, so you'll see where I'm coming from—"

"I do see." She picked up a pencil and rolled it between her forefinger and thumb. "And I wish I knew how to allay your fears and insecurities. How about this? It's not going to be easy, because it's not *supposed* to be easy."

I grinned at that.

"But," she went on, "and this is most important, I think you're potentially one of the finest athletes I've seen around here."

When she said that, I almost fell off my chair. I gripped the arms tightly to steady myself.

The coach looked at me intently. "I don't usually give out compliments like that, Megan, especially with a new girl. But I'm doing it because it's the truth as I see it, and because I believe you can handle the truth."

"Now you've made me more nervous than ever," I moaned.

"Rubbish!" She sounded stern and kind of

forbidding, and I wished I hadn't said that last thing. "Megan, you're just young, that's all. Young and nervous sometimes go together. But time will be on your side, and in a few weeks you'll be an old, experienced varsity player."

She stood up to show that our little talk was over, as far as she was concerned. "Any more questions?" she asked crisply.

"No, I guess not—"

"You won't get very many compliments from me, Megan," she said as a final statement. "Mostly you'll get a lot of criticism. But today— today was a little bit different."

"Thank you," I said, standing up. I felt a surge of energy run through me. Maybe it came from pride or some kind of crazy confidence, the kind I used to have years before when I knew I was better than the boys at Winchester Pond. Whatever it was, it felt good to have it back again.

I wasn't going to worry about Annemarie or those others calling me a hotshot. I'd show them. I'd *be* a hotshot, if that's what it took!

Chapter Nine

"First game of the season, hmm?" Troy said, sneaking up behind me as I stood at my locker. "You're playing against Sacred Heart High today. This is it, Meegles—the big time."

"Please," I said, turning to face him. "My heart is pounding hard enough as it is. Look at me, I'm à wreck."

"I'm looking," he said, his dark eyes dancing devilishly. "And you look pretty good to me."

I put out a hand and touched the collar of his shirt. He looked pretty good himself, in a blue button-down oxford shirt and black jeans. The pale blue made his eyes seem a deeper brown and his hair almost blue-black. Just looking at him made me go a little bit weak in the knees.

"None of that stuff in the halls, you two," Dave Waldon called out as he passed by, shaking his head as if shocked. "Disgraceful."

I laughed and pulled my hand away from Troy's collar.

"It's a home game," I said. "All of North High can watch me make a fool of myself as of two-thirty."

"You're going to be fine," Troy assured me. "But you may be right about the whole school being there. Even football practice has been suspended for an hour, so we can watch you play. Sometimes I think our coach is more interested in field hockey than football. Either that, or he's interested in Coach Mallen. Meg, don't look so nervous, I'll be there."

That made me feel even more nervous. I knew my mother was coming, too, and Beth.

As far as the actual playing went, I was still trying to feel confident in practice. I knew that from here on we'd have two games a week, usually, for a total of twenty games. We'd been practicing hard, and things had been going well. But a real game—that was something else.

The team from Sacred Heart High arrived at about two o'clock, and I watched them as they stepped down from their bus, one by one. Why was it that they all seemed to move with grace, strength, and total confidence?

I tried to convince myself that I would look that way someday, too. But deep inside it was hard to believe.

In the locker room, most of our team was already changing. Everyone seemed to be talking about the Sacred Heart team who'd made a pretty strong impression last season. I got out my uniform, which consisted of a really short maroon-and-gold plaid kilt, maroon panty-shorts underneath, and a trim, white knitted shirt. Our legs were covered with long tube socks and maroon shin guards. And then there were the cleated shoes.

I couldn't believe that I was getting into the varsity skirt instead of the plain maroon skirts the JV team wore. I felt like an imposter.

But at the same time I knew I looked good. I was tall and slim, and my legs would look OK in that short skirt. Just looking good wasn't much comfort, though, when I wanted to look like an athlete.

We left the locker room together, as a team, making a lot of psyching noises. "Stomp on Sacred Heart," someone would begin, and the rest of us would chant along, "Beat 'em, Raiders!"

The afternoon was cool and sunny, a pleasant change from all the hot August practice days. The wind ruffled our hair and skirts as we walked out onto the hockey field.

We didn't start the game as soon as we got there. While the coaches conferred with each other and the referees, all the players, varsity and junior varsity, formed a big circle. I noticed that the Sacred Heart girls did the same.

It was time for stretching and warm-ups, led by Gina, the varsity team captain. We placed our sticks down in front of us and went through the paces, chanting sometimes as we went. "Beat Sacred Heart! Defeat Sacred Heart!" I could hear the opposing team doing much the same thing over in their exercise circle.

Then the two captains went to meet the refs, and a coin was tossed to choose sides of the field. Sacred Heart won the toss, so they would go first in the game.

The captains came back for a huddle, which meant more screaming and cheering. The noise was wild. "We're gonna do it—We're gonna beat them!" we shouted over and over, and I felt my nerves give way to pure energy.

"Two, four, six, eight, who're we gonna eliminate?

"Sacred Heart! Yeah!!"

Now we were ready to play hockey.

Coach Mallen chose her starting lineup. Not surprisingly, I wasn't in it. I was sitting on the bench. Oh, well, what did I expect? A newcomer in the first game of the season?

They started the game with a pass-back in the center of the field. A Sacred Heart forward passed the ball backward to one of her teammates, who then put the ball in play with a swift pass. And the game was off.

Amazed by all the loud cheering, I took a good look at the sidelines. Our friends were there, as well as the football team already dressed for practice, parents, teachers, and most of the school staff, including the cafeteria and maintenance people. There were even a few people scurrying around with cameras and note pads.

I watched the game closely, leaning forward on the bench and jumping up now and then to follow the action back and forth on the sidelines. It didn't look so impossible. Yes, everyone on the field looked strong and lithe, but—

But I was dying to get out there!

"Hey, Meg," said Beth, coming over to me. "Just wanted to wish you luck."

"Thanks, Beth," I murmured, distracted. My eyes were scanning the field, watching as the Raiders' defense kept whacking the ball away from their goal cage. No one had scored yet.

"I can't believe how many people are watching this thing," Beth said. "Even your brother is here, but he's over with his newspaper friends, pretending he's not really interested in field hockey."

I turned to her, thinking again that maybe it was Mike she was interested in.

"Well, that's how Mike is," I said. "He has a hard time showing his emotions."

"I guess." She changed the subject. "I can't get over how many people turn out for these games. Field hockey is an absolute craze at this school. You're heading for the spotlight, Meg." With that, she gave me a hug and disappeared into the crowd.

The referees' whistles blew almost continually. Both teams seemed to be fouling left and right. And about fifteen minutes into the game, Tammy Lowell was limping as though she had pulled a muscle in her leg. The coach called me over.

"At the next break, Megan, you go in for Tammy. Right link."

This was it. I went to the timekeeper's table and said, "Substitution. Megan Carter for Tammy Lowell."

I put my mouth guard in place and followed the ref, as I was supposed to. I told her I was a substitute, and then I waited. Finally the whistle blew for someone's foul. I gripped my stick and ran as fast as I could; I had only ten seconds to get out there, and Tammy had only ten seconds to get off the field.

After I got into place, I looked around, flexing my arms and batting my stick against the ground for practice. This was unreal. It had to be. There were literally hundreds of spectators along the sidelines. With all those eyes watching, it seemed as though I would never remember how to play. I felt rooted to the spot.

All of a sudden I saw one special pair of eyes: Troy, holding his helmet under one arm, was giving me the high sign. He winked and made a circle with his forefinger and thumb, and I knew he was telling me that I'd do just fine.

I decided to just pretend I was on Winchester Pond again and I sent a "thank-you" grin to Troy.

It seemed only seconds after that when the ball, shot from a free hit, came zooming toward me. Talk about adrenaline! I sprang into action, going for the ball, steadying it, and then I began to dribble down the field. I was doing all right until a tall Sacred Heart fullback came charging at me.

No way, I thought in a frenzy and passed the

ball along to Gina. She was positioned in a perfect strategic spot and had taken the ball to the striking circle in seconds.

Gina aimed, took a fierce shot, and we all watched as the ball sailed into the goal cage. The goalie didn't know what had hit her. We had scored our first goal!!

For a moment, everyone—the team and our fans—went absolutely crazy, cheering and blowing whistles. Someone even clanged a loud cowbell.

The whole game wasn't full of great moments, but there were a lot of them. I was on a roll. I moved quickly, made some pretty decent decisions, and kept feeding passes to the forwards. We were ahead five to two at the end of the first half.

Exhausted, we went for cups of water and sucked on little bits of orange while we cooled off. The coach talked to us again, discussing strategy and priming us up for a win.

"And you, Megan," she said, pointing a finger at me. "Watch out for your rough play. You're coming awfully close to fouling—"

"But she gets the job done!" Gina put in, ignoring Coach Mallen's glare.

In the second half I really moved. I concentrated on not committing any fouls, but I charged around as though I owned the field. I stopped being afraid. I was there to make goals, and that's what I started to do.

One goal after another. The crowd started to howl, "Go, Raiders, go!" and that spurred me on even more.

Later Troy told me I was like a blur out there on the field, that I moved so fast he could hardly keep up with me. I don't know. I just did what I could, and I kept trying to do it better.

Before we finished, I'd scored three goals. Mine alone! The game whizzed by so fast that I didn't have time to think about what was happening. But when it was over, we had won twelve to four.

It was unbelievable. The crowds were shouting my name.

I stared, blinking my eyes in the sunlight, feeling the sweat dripping down my face. All those faces blurred together at the sidelines, so I couldn't tell Troy from my mother or Beth or Kelsey. I didn't even know who was cheering for me.

All I knew was that I had been recognized as a real hockey player.

We were still on the field, lining up to shake hands with the Sacred Heart team.

"Great game, Megan," said Gina, coming up behind me. "You really made the difference."

"Thanks. I just—" But before I could finish, I heard Annemarie and her crowd starting up again.

"She thinks she's so special."

"Little sophomore hotshot!"

"I never saw anyone try to steal the whole show like that. It's absolutely obnoxious!"

They weren't exactly mentioning my name, but there was no doubt that it was me they were talking about.

Don't let it hurt you, I told myself. *They're jealous.* But I could have talked to myself for six solid hours, and it wouldn't have done much good. It hurt being talked about that way.

"Don't let them get you down, Megan," Tammy whispered to me. "You were terrific. Just ignore them."

"Right," I mumbled. "Just ignore them."

After all the formalities of the game were finished, Troy came over, still holding his helmet.

"That was one fantastic game, Megan!" He looked at me, his dark eyes dancing, and I thought it was worth playing just to have this boy look at me like that. "You should hear how people are talking about you," he went on. "Everyone wanted to know who you were."

"Cut it out," I said. "You're teasing."

"Ask your brother. Hey, Mike, come here a minute."

Mike strolled over, looking amused.

"Weren't people asking who the new player is?" Troy said.

Mike hesitated for a minute. For him to actually give me a compliment always requires a major effort. But suddenly his face broke into a big grin. "They really were, Megan. It was wild. All these maniacs kept talking about you until—I think you've become a household word by now."

"Oh, Mike—"

"No exaggeration," my brother said. "You exploded in that game. I even had to give your name to a couple of reporters from the newspapers. The real newspapers, not the school paper."

I gulped.

"And Mom is thrilled beyond all reason," he added. "She's over there with all the other hockey mothers, beaming like crazy." Now Mike got that teasing expression on his face. "The only one I'm worried about is Troy, here. It may not be easy going out with North High's new superstar."

Confused, I turned to Troy. "Is that true?" I whispered.

"No, of course not." Troy laughed. "You're a star, all right, but I think I can handle that.

What I can't handle is what Coach Riley is going to do to me if I don't get over to football practice. See you later, champ."

Suddenly I felt exhausted. Too much was happening. The game itself. Reporters. Fans cheering for me. The remarks from Annemarie's friends. And now the sinking feeling that Mike might be right. What if all this was hard on Troy?

I was feeling dizzy, exhilarated, and a million other things that I couldn't get a grasp on.

Chapter Ten

Absolutely nothing was the same after that.

When our local newspaper came out on Friday morning, there were pictures of me all over the sports pages.

"New Sports Star Is Born," was the first headline I saw as I was trying to swallow my cereal. I almost choked. Mike walked into the kitchen holding up the paper as though it were kind of a banner.

"Behold," he said. "A full page of Megan Carter, Girl Wonder. A legend in her own time—"

"What do you mean? It doesn't say that—" I leaped up from the breakfast table and made a grab for the paper.

"No, it doesn't say exactly that, but it might

as well." Mike unfolded the paper so that all of us could read it at once.

It was creepy, all those pictures of me when I hadn't even known that anyone's camera was aimed at me. They had shots of me soaring down the field toward Sacred Heart's goal cage, and pictures of me taking a giant swing at the ball, with my stick poised above my shoulder. Perfect form. I could barely believe it was me.

"Carter's as fast as the *Concorde*," read the caption. "And she makes her own rules at times."

"Wow," I said in a breathless voice.

"Right," Mike said. "I spoke to that guy, the sports reporter for the *Sentinel*. Hey, they only send him out to important games, lady. They consider Coach Mallen's varsity games to be really big news these days."

I stared at all those pictures. The write-up was even more wild. It said things like, "Megan Carter, the new natural, has been described by her coach as an 'awesome player,' especially for one so young . . . Carter and Company thoroughly pounced on Sacred Heart to end with a 12–4 finish. . . ."

"Carter and Company?" I whispered, suddenly horrified. Wasn't I having enough trouble with Annemarie and her crowd? I could still hear their taunts. This newspaper spread would really finish me with them. In fact, the whole team would have good reason to hate me.

I began to feel sick to my stomach. I turned away from the newspaper and clutched at my middle, wondering if I could stay home from school for the day.

"What's the matter, Megan?" my mother asked. "You don't look very well. Are you sick?"

"Yeah. I am. I think I'm going to throw up."

My mother sat me down and looked into my eyes, as if searching for signs of fever or concussion.

"I just want to stay home today," I said, trying to sound convincingly sick.

"Megan." My mother fixed her eyes on mine. "Now what is it that's troubling you? The newspaper story?"

I lowered my eyes. "They had no right to make such a fuss about me when everyone played a good game—"

"This is a very good article, Megan," my dad remarked from behind the paper. "It shouldn't upset you. Why, I had a lot of stories written about me when I was an all-star at college."

"You said you wanted to make a name for yourself," Jessica reminded me. She was right. I could have killed her for it.

"Of course, the other girls played well," Mike put in. "But you were the only *new* girl. And a sophomore, at that."

"Will you all please stop?" I howled. "Can't

you just listen to me for a minute? I'm having trouble with—with some of the seniors on the team. They don't like me. They already think I'm a 'hotshot and a show-off.' Quote, unquote. Now, with this thing in the paper—this Carter and Company stuff—they'll really be mad."

"Oh." It seemed as if everyone in my family had said "Oh" at the same exact time.

"Look, maybe it's only natural," my mom ventured, "that those seniors would resent someone new, *and* someone younger, coming in and making all those goals right away."

"Three goals! Three!" Jessie reminded us.

"But they'll get over it," my mom went on. "After all, they'll get to know you as a person before long."

"They'll never give me a chance, especially after this," I said. "I'm just a sophomore to them, and I just started—"

My father put a hand on my shoulder. "You have to realize, Megan, that life is not a popularity contest. In other words, you can't please all of the people all of the time."

I groaned. If there's one thing I can't stand, it's wise old sayings when I'm falling apart.

"Very true," Mike said philosophically. "You're bound to make a few enemies at first, but—hey, those troublemakers will be graduating after this year, anyway. So think of it that way. They'll be gone, they'll be history."

"Doesn't help much this season," I said glumly.

"It's not easy getting all this sudden attention," my mother acknowledged. "But you can handle it, Megan. You'll find your own way, in your own time."

I blinked back tears that had formed because my family cared so much. Most of my psychology articles had said that the Middle Child usually gets the least attention in a family group. It was beginning to occur to me that they might be wrong.

So maybe every cloud does have some sort of a silver lining, I thought. Jessica reached over and patted my hand lovingly. I decided that she was a pretty terrific little sister, after all.

"May I have your autograph, Miss Carter?"

Troy and his car, the Brown Monster, were waiting outside my house when I finally got my act together and left for school.

"What are you doing here?" I asked, feeling all lit up inside.

"I came to give you a ride to school." As usual he looked great. The sunlight was playing off his sleek, dark hair, and he was wearing his maroon-and-gold varsity football sweater. "A little birdie told me you needed some cheering up," he said teasingly.

"Who?" My mouth fell open in surprise. "Mike?"

"Yeah, he called me a little while ago. Said maybe you were a victim of too much newspaper hype."

"Well, did you read that terrible stuff?" I demanded, getting into his car.

"Sure. This town needs a sports hero, Meg, and you seem to be it. After all, there's nobody outstanding in boys' sports."

I scrunched down in the front seat of his car while he started up the motor.

"I don't know, Troy. I used to think I wanted to be sort of famous, but—I've decided, fame is for the birds."

He put out a hand and held mine in his warm, strong grip. "So the senior girls are being a bunch of major creeps. So what?"

"Mike told you about that, too?"

"Your brother's very thorough when it comes to reporting the news. Besides, we juniors tend to understand more about the politics of sports."

I found myself grinning. "Oh, really?"

"You're going to be OK, Meegles. You've just got to hang in there and do what's right. They'll learn, after a while, that you're not trying to grab all the newspaper publicity." He hesitated for a minute. "You're not, are you?"

"How can you even ask?" I was furious. "I was just playing as well as I could. I never even talked to a reporter."

Troy sat there silently, staring at me.

"You do believe me, don't you, Troy?"

"Yeah," he said after a small hesitation. "I do. You keep playing the way you have been. And don't let anyone stop you."

Looking at Troy, I started to wonder what I was worrying about. I was sitting there with the greatest guy I had ever known. The day was gorgeous. The air smelled sharp and Septemberish, sort of like apples, leaf fires, and pumpkins.

I felt some of the tension drain out of me.

"Thanks, Troy," I whispered.

"You're very welcome." He moved a few inches closer and grazed my mouth very gently with his lips. It was such a soft, light kiss that it should have been nothing. But the sheer joy of it stayed with me all day long.

At school the craziness was everywhere. It seemed everyone had read the sports page that morning and had something to say.

"Wow, you must have played a great game, Megan," I was told by dozens of kids and quite a few teachers.

"Good work," people I didn't even know said as they passed me in the halls.

And a lot of them said things like, "I'll have to get to more of the field hockey games. It's the best team in the school. . . ."

At lunch three guys from the football team, all carrying trays of food, passed by me in the cafeteria and yelled, "Hey! If it isn't the sophomore sensation herself!"

I guess I started to enjoy it. Pretty soon I had forgotten my stomachache and my worries about Annemarie and her friends. This was what I had been dreaming about—finding something I was really good at and becoming known for it. Besides, I told myself, I had worked hard at field hockey and earned the attention—hadn't I?

I sailed through all my classes that day—the world sharp and clear. Everything looked larger than life. I began to think it was because I felt like a new person. First of all, a big weight had been lifted from my shoulders. With my mom at home again, I wasn't responsible for the laundry, the vacuuming, and the dirty dishes. Nobody was complaining to me about being out of clean socks. I even found my bed made up for me every afternoon when I arrived home from practice.

Second, I had Troy now, and that was like some kind of dream come true.

And above all, of course, I was being heralded by the newspapers and the whole school as a sports star.

Right after lunch I sneaked into the home ec

room, where there was a full-length mirror for the sewing class. I stared at the person who was supposed to be Megan Carter.

I saw the same tall, slim girl with dark curls. I saw an outfit that belonged to me, the straight-leg jeans and the oversize red-and-blue jungle-patterned shirt. My red flat shoes. My little gold earrings.

Yeah, it seemed to be me, all right. Yet everything around me was so different. People were noticing me. Newspapers had published photos of me. I was a star. And I felt different.

Sophomore year had barely begun, and yet it had already changed me. I took one last look at my reflection and gave myself a little hug, wondering what other changes this year would bring.

Chapter Eleven

On Saturday Kelsey, Beth, and I went to North High's football game against Litchwood. We sat right in the front row, where we could really watch the game. None of us knew much about football, but we were determined to learn.

It seemed as if the whole school had turned out for the first game of the season. North High is definitely a sports-minded school, even though the football team hasn't been very good in recent years. Anyway, it was a major event, and I was pretty excited since I hadn't been able to go to any of the games the year before.

We all wore bright maroon sweatshirts that said "Raiders" on them and maroon ribbons in our hair. Dave had even given us big "Win,

Raiders" buttons that Kelsey pinned to our sweatshirts.

"Now let's try to figure out what those guys are doing out there," I said to my friends. "Troy drew a diagram of the football field for me." I pulled out the paper and unfolded it. We all stared at the strange, weird marks Troy had made on the paper.

"It's nothing like a hockey field, is it?" Kelsey asked, looking at it with a shrug.

"I know one thing," Beth said. "The quarterback is really important to the game. He's sort of the leader of the offense. That's him right there—Brad Kellogg."

"OK. That's cool," I said, squinting to see way out on the field. All I could make out were those gigantic uniforms that made every boy look like King Kong. There was a lot of crashing around. Then there were piles of players all in a big, dangerous-looking heap. It seemed like an impossible game to figure out.

"Can I be of any help?" My brother Mike came up behind us, taking a seat on the bleachers.

"Only if you can decipher this game," said Beth. She turned and focused all her attention on my brother. "We can't figure out what the quarterback does—or anyone else, for that matter." (*Ah-ha*, I thought. Just as I had suspected! Beth was interested in Mike!)

"No problem," Mike said, taking the diagram Troy had drawn. "You see, it's different from hockey because in football there are two groups of players on each team," he began.

We all nodded and took another look at Troy's mysterious diagram. Between Troy's diagram and Mike's complicated explanation of who did what and how they all did it in downs, I was beginning to grasp the basic principles of the game—sort of. For a moment I pictured myself "talking football" with Troy—a good idea but probably something that was not about to happen in the immediate future. It was all I could do to figure out what was going on out on the field. If someone had asked me, I would have said, "I think they're getting creamed."

Meanwhile, I had something else on my mind. I couldn't help noticing that Beth hung on Mike's every word. She was infatuated with him—my brother!

For the rest of the game Mike continued to give us pointers on the action. When I say "us," however, I really mean Beth, because it was beginning to be obvious that he was noticing her, too.

I thought that was pretty neat. They had a lot in common, both of them liked to read a lot, and write, and they both wanted to be journalists. My brain started buzzing. I would have to see what I could do to help this along.

The game ended with North High's Raiders taking a terrible trouncing, as usual. Litchwood simply had a better team, and no matter how hard our guys tried, they never even got near the goal. Brad Kellogg, our quarterback, seemed to get sacked every time he moved. I knew Troy was waiting to run with the passes, but the one that actually came toward him was intercepted by Litchwood. The final score was a pitiful thirteen to nothing.

The North High fans were dejected, but not really surprised. It probably would have been a shock if our team *had* won.

"Are you going to write up the game for the paper?" Beth asked my brother.

"No, I never do sports stories," Mike said, looking pleased that she had asked. "I'd rather write my critical essays."

Beth nodded. "I liked that one you did last year about students' rights. You're really good at putting your arguments down on paper—"

"And he knows it, too," I interrupted, teasing Mike as usual.

"Look who's talking." Mike glared at me. "Miss Publicity herself."

"Oh, knock it off," I said. "Half of the information in those newspaper stories came from you, and you know it."

Mike looked suddenly serious and put a brotherly hand square on my head. "Yeah, Megan, I know," he said kindly. "I only hope Troy is convinced of it, too."

Troy and I had a movie date that night. When he came to pick me up, I was still trying to decide between a blue cotton skirt and my jeans. I finally decided on the skirt and a white blouse edged with lace.

"Sorry to hear about the game," my dad was saying to Troy when I finally emerged from my room. They were in the recreation room, which is where we usually watch television. My mother was out, visiting with the Hardins next door.

"Thanks. I guess it's the same old story," Troy said, sounding a little downhearted.

"Well, I'm sure you'll do better in future games," my father said optimistically. "After all, you have a lot of big guys on the team." I winced. What kind of comfort was that supposed to be?

"That's not the problem," Troy told him honestly. "We don't seem to have the team solidarity, for some reason. Not like the field hockey team. They all pull together."

"Hi," I said, walking in. "How're you doing?"

"Oh, great. Fine," Troy said glumly. "Superfine, after a score like that today."

My father sat down to watch his show again. "Oh, they'll win next time, Megan, you just wait and see," he proclaimed.

"I guess your dad's an optimist," Troy said, trying not to sound cynical. But I knew that he was feeling pretty low.

I pulled my blue corduroy jacket out of the coat closet, and we headed for the door. "An incurable optimist," I confirmed.

"What movie do you want to see?" he asked.

"Doesn't matter to me," I said. "Something light and funny, I think. From the looks of you, you don't need any nuclear holocausts or multiple murder stories."

"Right." He gave me a wry smile. "A comedy it will be, then. I know just the one. Good night, Mr. Carter."

"Good night, Troy. And cheer up. Next week'll be different."

"Obviously, he didn't see us play today," Troy muttered as we went out the door.

The movie didn't cheer Troy up much. Although he did do a pretty good job of hiding his depression. Truthfully, it was a lousy film.

Afterward we wound up sitting in Troy's car on Main Street, in front of the drugstore, talking about how terrible the movie had been.

We sat there, feeling cozy and easy and in no hurry to drive away. From where we sat, you could look up Main Street and see the whole town green. The green is an expanse of grass that goes all the way from Bridge Street up three blocks to the hospital. It's actually very pretty. There are maples planted every twenty feet or so for shade, and in December they put up a line of evergreens strung with lights.

Troy leaned his head back against the headrest. "You make me feel better whenever I'm down, Megan."

"Good," I said. "Because you've been there for me when I needed cheering up."

He closed his eyes for a second. "Do you suppose that's what real caring is? Just—being there for each other? Being more concerned about the other person's troubles than your own?"

My heart seemed to skip a few beats. "Sounds like a good definition to me."

"Megan, I'm sorry I was sort of bummed out tonight," Troy said. "It's not my style, really. I just get discouraged because—oh, because we train so hard, and Riley's a good coach, and we have all the ingredients for a good football team—and yet we don't seem to have the right stuff."

"I know. I saw how hard you tried, all of you. It must be tough."

He ran his hand through his thick, dark hair. "It gets so frustrating. I wish I knew how not to let it get to me."

I had an inspiration. "Well, I have something for you that might help," I announced, opening my purse and rummaging through it. "Ah. Here it is. I found it in my desk, just for you."

Troy looked at it, and then at me, as though I were a nut case. "What in the world *is* it?"

"An article by Dr. Jane Pembroke."

He stared again at the tattered piece of magazine. "Dr. Who?"

I pointed to the title of the piece. "Look, there. This was her article called 'Coping with Failure.' It makes a lot of sense, Troy. She really gets into a situation like yours, where the failure isn't your own fault but a combination of circumstances that—"

"This article is dated two years ago," Troy said in disbelief. "Where did you get this thing, anyway?"

"In a magazine, naturally. Where else?"

"But—two years later? I don't understand, Megan."

"Well, I have a collection of articles. Psychology articles. I've been cutting them out for years because they really tell a person how to handle things in life—"

I stopped because of the way he was looking at me.

"You're kidding me, right?" he asked.

"No," I said indignantly. "I'm not kidding at all."

"You mean to tell me you learn about life by

reading this—this—" He glanced down at the name. "This Dr. Jane Pembroke?"

"That's right. And if you laugh, I'll never speak to you again."

He put up a hand defensively. "No, no, I'm not laughing. At least, I'm trying not to. Megan, I just think it's kind of cute, that's all—cutting out these articles. Just how many do you have, anyway?"

I thought about that. "I don't know. Probably about three hundred. Not all by Dr. Jane Pembroke, of course—"

"Oh. I see." He was biting his lip.

"Don't get that look on your face!" I said, trying to stay outraged. "You look as though you're humoring me."

"I don't mean to. Really. I think it's pretty adorable, actually. Do you have all these in a scrapbook or something?"

"No," I said and sniffed. "In files. Neatly marked file folders, by subject."

"By subject?"

"Yes. Under *A*, I have Aberrations, Anxiety, and Agoraphobia—"

"What in the heck are those???"

"You see? I am much better educated than you, because of Dr. Jane Pembroke—"

"What do you have under *B*? Bonkers? Bonehead? Bozos?"

I giggled. "Blink-brain," I said. And then we were both laughing, laughing hard, letting off a lot of steam and just plain breaking the ice between us.

"I'm glad I found out about this—this aberration of yours," he said.

"I'll kill you if you tell—"

"That would go under *H*, for Hostility."

"Troy—" I was laughing helplessly.

"Come on, Megan, I'm not really making fun of you. Hey, whatever you have to do in this life that helps you to cope, I'm all for it."

He looked at the paper I'd given him. "It's just too bad I'm such a failure that you felt you had to give this to me," he said in a quiet, flat voice.

"Oh, Troy, no. You're not! Your team is, but—" I stopped. Maybe no matter what I said, it would be the wrong thing.

So instead of talking, I leaned over and kissed him gently on his cheek.

Chapter Twelve

We had a field hockey game on Tuesday, about twenty miles away, in the town of Westcliff. The JV and varsity teams went by bus, of course, and they had a special bus for fans, which was completely filled with kids from North High. There was also a caravan of loyal parents who drove over in cars to Westcliff High, the same parents who were always there with the cow-bells and other noisemakers for cheering. As a result of all this, when we arrived at Westcliff, we probably had more fans than the home team.

As I said, our school is very sports minded.

Coach Mallen gave us our pregame talk out in the circle on Westcliff's field. She stressed team spirit and working together as she had at the last game. Then when she had left the circle, Gina also talked about pulling together out on the field.

Annemarie, standing a few people away from me, said rather loudly, "*Some* people ought to learn the art of passing, instead of trying to steal the whole show." She stared straight at me, and so did her pals.

I felt myself shrinking and getting smaller by the minute. I didn't know enough about the game to be able to talk back to her.

But Gina did, and she turned quickly to Annemarie.

"Some other people ought to learn the art of *being there* to be passed to," she snapped. "If Megan or any other player needs to pass, and you're off somewhere looking at the pleats in your kilt, then she's going to charge ahead and make the goal by herself."

Annemarie looked furious but didn't reply. I could tell, though, that she was madder than ever.

Actually, Annemarie was a good player, and she never spent a minute worrying about the pleats in her skirt. But it was true that she didn't always keep up in the running department. She had a tendency to tire easily, and everyone knew she resented anyone who was consistently energetic.

That day's game was hard. Westcliff had a really strong team, and we had to hustle to keep them from scoring against us.

Ours was a team that was accustomed to winning. North High had been winning division championships for at least five years now. Because of Coach Mallen's training, we knew how to pull together and play good hockey— even if there were personal resentments among us.

But by the second half I was really feeling the hostility of Annemarie and her friends. Only now it wasn't just those three. There was definite resentment coming from a few girls in the junior class, too. It seemed as though nobody wanted to pass to me, speak to me, or even look at me.

Of course, that made me all the more aggressive. I remembered the boys back at Winchester Pond and how hard I'd tried to get their acceptance. It finally did come, but grudgingly.

So, I ignored the treatment I got from my teammates. Trying to conquer my frustration, I went charging around like a maniac, taking the ball from the opposition in any way I legally could. And to be honest, maybe all my methods weren't legal. I wasn't always sure. But often I was so fast that the refs didn't see everything.

At the end, the score was fourteen to six in our favor, and again I'd scored three of the goals myself.

The crowds were still on my side, shouting my name and cheering me on, but my own teammates weren't doing it this time. It was bizarre. Even the Westcliff team noticed. I heard one of their girls whispering, "She's the best player I've ever seen, but nobody on her team likes her."

And then, getting changed in the visitors' locker room, it seemed that only Kelsey was really my friend. The others kept their distance.

The unseen voices started up just as I was slipping into my sweatpants. "I don't know why she doesn't just go off and join some college varsity team," said someone from the other side of the row of lockers.

"Right. She's obviously much too talented for the likes of this team!" That had to be Allison.

I felt myself going hot and cold all over. My emotions were in such a whirl, I didn't know what I was feeling—anger, shame, despair, or what. But my heart felt really heavy, as though there were a giant stone attached to it.

Annemarie's voice rang out, even louder than the other's.

"Maybe we could have a statue erected on our

school's front lawn. Megan Carter, Girl Wonder." There was a chorus of snickers. "Then everyone could bow down and worship the statue on their way to school each morning."

I slammed my locker shut.

"I don't think I can take much more of this," I said to Kelsey.

"What do you mean?" Kelsey asked. "You're not going to quit the team, are you?"

"No, I'm not a quitter. I read an article once that said quitting can become a habit that's very hard to break—" I stopped. I didn't feel like explaining all my psychology articles to Kelsey right then.

But that started me thinking. What would Dr. Jane Pembroke have said about the situation that I was in? I sat there on the bench, wishing Dr. Jane had one of those call-in radio shows, so that I could telephone her.

"Hi, you're on the air," she'd say.

"Hi. I'm Megan, and I'm fifteen."

"Hello, Megan. And what is your problem?"

"Dr. Jane, I've looked in my files under Jealousy and Hatred and Rejection, because that's what I'm getting from some of the older girls on my field hockey team, but I can't seem to find the answer anywhere—"

Of course Dr. Jane would stop me right there

and make me explain my problem in more specific terms.

But then my imagination balked. What would Dr. Jane say about my problem?

Suddenly I knew. She always advised people to *do* something, rather than just let a problem continue. It was better to take a shot at solving the problem than to just sit there hoping the whole thing would go away.

Well, there was no reason not to take her advice, even though she hadn't actually given it to me. I stood up before I could lose my nerve.

Kelsey eyed me nervously. "Megan, what are you—?"

But I didn't answer her. I just marched myself around the lockers. Annemarie sat on the long wooden bench, looking pretty and extremely cool with her blond ponytail. Her friends, stood around her, staring at me as though I were a bug that needed to be squashed.

"Look, I need to get something off my chest," I began.

Mistake. I should have known that would bring a few snickers from the senior section.

"Her chest—what chest?" Allison whispered loudly.

But I forged ahead, anyway.

"You guys," I said. "You know I can hear everything you're saying about me. And you must know that you're making me feel totally lousy."

"Oooh, poor baby," Annemarie said.

"You can be as rude as you want," I said, staring straight at Annemarie and her gang. "But I have to say this. I know I'm the newest member of the team, and the youngest. But that is not my doing. *I didn't put myself there.* All I wanted to do was make junior varsity, but this is the way things worked out."

Annemarie was squirming, just as I'd hoped she would.

"Why do you always do so much showing off, then?" demanded Sue.

"Showing off? Is it showing off to play your best?" I felt my face turning all red, but I just stared at Sue. "Do you want me to play like a total klutz, just so maybe people will like me?"

"Get to the point, hotshot," Annemarie said, yawning.

"Sure." I stared at her now. "The point is, I can't go on being treated like an outcast. If I'm going to be the local leper, then I might as well hang up my shin guards right now."

Nobody said a word to that. They just looked at me with intense interest.

"Come on," I said. "Give me a break, will you? I thought you wanted a winning team. So I play my hardest, trying to help us win."

"We do want to win," Sue said. "But you—you're always trying to make us look bad."

"No, I'm not," I said flatly. "I look up to you seniors, and I try to learn from you. Is it my fault that I learned to play hockey with boys years ago? That I became an aggressive player?"

"No, that's not your fault, Megan," Allison said slowly. Annemarie glared at her. "Well, we never thought of it that way," Allison explained. Now a small crowd was starting to gather around us.

"And how is any of this back stabbing helping the team?" asked Gina, sounding official in her capacity as team captain. There were at least seven girls gathered around us now.

"It's not," Sue said, looking a tiny bit ashamed.

"Thank you," I whispered. I could feel tears springing into my eyes, and I sure didn't want that! Quickly I brushed them away.

"We do want to win," said Lisa Kennett, a junior. "And maybe we were a little bit jealous of your abilities, but—we're sorry. At least, I know I am."

"Ditto," agreed Sue and Allison. Annemarie, I noticed, said nothing, but she was looking somewhat less hateful.

Oh, well, I couldn't win them all.

I walked away, still trembling and still fighting off my tears. But they were definitely tears of relief. I had faced a problem head on, taking a really big gamble—and this time, it seemed, I had won!

"Way to go, Megan," Kelsey whispered, giving me a friendly nudge in the ribs.

Chapter Thirteen

"Mom, may Mike and I give a party in the recreation room some Friday or Saturday night?" I threw this at my mother one day after practice. She and I were sitting outside on the lawn chairs in the backyard, enjoying what was left of the late-September afternoon.

"A party," she repeated, looking skeptical. "Hmmm, I never expected that— Well, why not? As long as it's not too huge, and as long as you know that your father and I will remain in the house as chaperones."

"Oh, of course. And as for the number of kids, just a few of Mike's friends and a few of mine."

Mom looked at me intently. "Not the whole hockey team?"

"No," I said. "I mean, some of them are becoming pretty good friends, but, no, I still wouldn't want to invite everyone. Not to this party, anyway. This would be primarily for couples, I think."

"Oh? And is Mike a 'couple' with someone?"

I laughed and pulled a blade of grass out of the lawn. "Not yet," I said. "But I'm hoping. What I mean by that is, he's attracted to a certain friend of mine—"

"Beth?"

My mouth fell open in surprise. "You knew about that?"

"I guessed it, the last time Beth was here," Mom smiled mysteriously. "She kept looking around for Mike, and once she even picked up his coffee cup and looked at it kind of dreamily for a minute."

We both laughed out loud.

"You see what I'm up against?" I asked. "Neither of them will do anything about it, they're both so shy."

"Creative types," my mother said, stretching lazily. "They don't always know how to handle anything romantic."

"You sound like Dr. Jane Pembroke," I said approvingly.

"Do I? No, I'm just plain old Mrs. Ralph Carter." She sounded sort of wistful.

"Mom, what's wrong?"

"Oh, Megan. You are perceptive. You're the one who should end up with a Ph.D. or a medical degree in psychiatry. You'll be the next Dr. Pembroke—"

"I don't understand. Are you unhappy with your new life, Mom?"

She brushed a lock of brown hair out of her eyes. She looked pretty that day, wearing a pair of brown cotton slacks and an oversize beige sweater with a cable pattern.

"The house and typing business aren't enough, after all?" I asked, probing gently.

"I guess you hit the nail on the head, Dr. Jane." She gave a short little laugh. "It's funny, really. I couldn't *wait* to get out of that factory so I could do things for my family, and free you so you could have a real life. . . ."

"I don't understand, then."

Mom sighed deeply. "OK. I have an awful lot of time on my hands. I've washed every window in the house, scrubbed and waxed every floor, tried every recipe in the *Passionate Joy of Cooking* book, and typed two dissertations this week—and still I don't feel busy enough."

"Oh. That's because you were used to going in ultra-high gear when you worked at the factory."

"Right. So now I feel like I'm stalled in neutral here."

I was really surprised. Who would have expected that my mom would actually miss her hectic old life?

"What—what are you going to do, Mom?"

A small smile played at the corners of her mouth. "Well, I'd like to go back to college."

My mouth dropped open. "Wow! What would you study?"

"Accounting," she said without hesitation.

"Terrific. Is that something you've always wanted?"

She nodded. "Yes, it is. But I think my going full-time would be a hardship on the family, right now."

"So—you can start out part-time and see how that goes. I think it's just super, Mom—if you want my opinion." A thought came to me that seemed terribly important. "You know what? I think having a degree would mean you'd never have to go back to a job on an assembly line again, no matter what."

"Exactly," she said. I could see that she really liked the idea. And who could blame her?

"Enough loafing," she said, standing up. "I've got a chicken dinner to prepare. And you can give me a hand, young lady."

"Me?" I yelped. "After a day of school and a long, hard hockey practice?"

"Yes, you. In case you didn't know it, your

brother and sister have been filling in for you for weeks now."

"What?"

"Right. They've been making your bed for you, cleaning your room, taking out the garbage, and picking up the yard—"

"All the things I used to do," I argued.

"Well, they've been darn good about it. Maybe only because I've been here to prod them, but still, they've been making life easier for you."

"I didn't know that," I said, suddenly touched. "Mike and Jessie, doing all those chores because they care about me? Hey, that's really nice of them."

"It is. And maybe it's time you pulled your weight again, too. At least now and then, to show your good faith."

I grinned. "All right. Watch my good faith." I stood up. "Lead me to the potato peeler."

We linked arms as we walked toward the back door. For the moment it felt as though we were two friends rather than mother and daughter.

I liked that feeling.

Chapter Fourteen

So I put my party plan into gear, setting the date for the first Saturday in October. My brother was surprised, to say the least, to hear that we were giving a party. But he soon got to like the idea, and he began to help me with the guest list. If he suspected my motives for giving the party, he never mentioned it. Beth didn't suspect, either, I don't think.

He invited some guys, his pals from the school newspaper, because he knew I'd be asking a few of my closest friends from the hockey team. He also surprised me by pitching in to get the basement room cleaned up.

"I can't believe this," I said the day before the party, when I was dusting the bookshelves. "My big brother actually knows how to clean something around the house?"

"None of your snide remarks," Mike tossed back at me. He was scrubbing some spots on the stairway carpeting. "You could ruin my reputation, you know."

"I really think it's great, Mike," I said sincerely. "A man of the eighties should be prepared to help with housework."

Mike looked up at me with a sort of tired, melodramatic expression. "I've been getting lots of practice," he said with a sigh. "Now that you're so busy with field hockey, Mom has Jessica and me doing dozens of chores every day."

"So I heard. I guess I ought to thank you both. I mean, everybody's been covering just so I can be free to concentrate on my hockey."

"I just hope you're not getting a swelled head, Megan." Mike said, amusement in his tone.

"Oh, come on," I said.

"Well, all those newspaper stories keep on praising you. You're the fastest-rising star this town has ever seen. It must be hard to maintain a balanced attitude, with a string of photographers always running after you."

"Don't you worry about that," I told him. "My feet are firmly on the ground."

But I wondered, just a little bit, if there was any truth to his words. I *had* been getting an awful lot of publicity lately, more than any other sports player in the school. And it was sort of exhilarating, the way people came up to me—not just at school, but everywhere in town—to say, "Good work, Megan. Keep it up." Sometimes, when I was with Troy, it became really awkward because the football team still hadn't won a game.

Later that evening Troy came over to help set up the party. He arrived with a folding table that we were going to use for Mike's big stereo set.

"I think it's comical," he said when Mike had gone upstairs to take a phone call. "You're giving this thing just to bring Beth and your brother together. Suppose it doesn't work?"

"Then we'll keep trying," I said. "I never give up, and I always get results. Don't you know that by now? I just keep going until I get what I want." I grinned. "Even if it's only a field hockey goal."

Troy looked at me in a strange way for a moment, and then shook his head and said, "As long as you remember that Beth and Mike aren't part of a hockey game."

'That's not the point." I turned to attack the basement windows with a cleaning solution. "I'm talking about not giving up—on anything. Like the way I talked to Annemarie and her friends that day in the locker room. That turned out better than I ever hoped."

"Yeah," Troy said in a flat voice. "You're one heck of a dynamo, all right."

I turned to look at him, but he was kneeling by the table, straightening its legs, and I couldn't read his face. "Was I just being obnoxious?" I asked hesitantly.

"A little," he returned with a grin.

"Sorry."

"Don't worry about it." He stood up and came over to me. "You smell like lemon wax."

"I wonder why? There's still so much to do, and Mike and I have been at it all day."

"No problem," he said, "you won't give up until you get what you want—even if it's just a clean basement. Listen, I've got to go. I promised my folks I'd put in an appearance at a family dinner. Some uncle I've never met is leaving for Europe or something."

"OK," I said. "I'll see you tomorrow night."

"See you then." He ran his hand through my hair, but he didn't kiss me, and as I watched him walk up the stairs I wondered if things really were OK.

Troy hadn't even mentioned the football team in the last two weeks. He was still playing, and they were still losing. He seemed resigned now rather than dejected as he had in the beginning of the season. And yet he came to hockey games whenever he could, and he was definitely one of our biggest fans. We had had six wins and no losses, and I was making goals at every game. Troy was almost always there afterward, whirling me off the ground for a celebration hug. Occasionally he became really quiet when the reporters came around, but that didn't seem so unusual. They could make anyone tongue-tied. No, when I thought about it, things were OK between us.

The Saturday of the party was crisp and cool—it was beginning to feel like Halloween weather. I spent most of the day fixing food and the basement with Mike and Beth.

I kept trying to get Mike to talk to Beth, or vice versa, but they were both so shy with each other. About the only thing they'd talk about was books. Naturally, I brought up every title I'd ever heard of, whether or not I'd read it.

"Have you read *Dune*, Beth? That's one of Mike's favorites, and I've been meaning to get to it." And then they'd discuss that for a few minutes while I conveniently went into another room. But as far as I could tell, no real chemistry was happening yet.

At one point, I even tried strategic timing. I sent them both to the broom closet at the same time to get the vacuum cleaner. They were each coming from a different direction—because that's the way I'd planned it—and they bumped into each other at the door.

"Ooops," Mike said.

"Oh, I'm so sorry," Beth said.

"Are you OK?"

I could hear all that polite conversation going on, but that was as far as it went.

"Well, if you don't need me anymore," Mike said, sort of uncomfortably, "maybe I'll go over to the school for a while. See how the football team is doing."

So that was the end of Mike for the afternoon. Beth and I continued to work away, making stacks of grinder sandwiches, cupcakes, and a giant salad.

All the hard work paid off. By eight o'clock that night the basement looked positively festive. The mounds of food we had prepared were all set out, and there were tubs of soda sitting in ice. Almost everyone who arrived had brought along a favorite album, so we had a great mix.

Kelsey and Dave were the first to arrive, followed by Tammy and Brad Kellogg, and then four guys from the *Echo.* Everyone wore jeans, as usual, and most kids wore big, colorful sweaters, and sneakers, of course.

Gina appointed herself temporary DJ, and

there was plenty of fast dancing, but none of it was helping the "romance" along.

"Mike hasn't gone near Beth yet," I whispered to Troy after one of the faster songs when everyone seemed to be out on the floor. "I've got to do something about this."

I walked past Kelsey and Dave. "How are you two doing?" I asked.

"Great," Kelsey replied, snuggling up to Dave quite happily. "Hey, did you hear about the football game this afternoon—?"

"No, but I don't have time right now," I said. "Tell me later. I have to play some nice dreamy music so maybe a certain brother of mine will ask a certain girl to dance."

I left them and went into conference with Gina. Together, we found the perfect record, a nice, slow love song, and put it on. If Mike didn't take the hint now, he was completely hopeless.

"Dance with me?" I asked Troy. He'd been looking sort of lost ever since he arrived—not his usual style at all. He took me in his arms, and we began to dance, and I realized I hadn't seen him smile all evening.

"Megan, have you—" he began, but at that moment I saw that my plan wasn't working.

"Look at Mike," I moaned. "Will you please do something for me? Will you go over and tell

Mike he should dance this one? That it's important for the host to set a good example, or something?"

"Sure." Troy released me and did just as I'd asked, and the next thing we knew, Mike finally walked over and said something to Beth. I could hardly believe it. They sort of smiled tentatively, like a pair of old friends who had suddenly found each other after years of separation.

I was so intent on watching them that I didn't even notice that Troy had come up behind me. "I guess your strategy is working," he said.

"Of course. They were made for each other. It's practically written in the stars."

"I don't think the stars have anything to do with it," he said dryly. "Megan Carter decided they belonged together, and their fate was as good as sealed."

"What?" I whirled around, hoping to see that he was kidding, but his dark eyes were serious. The fan light on the ceiling was revolving slowly, making light patterns flicker across the whole room, and for the first time I was aware of the shadows it made. I kept looking at Troy thrown into shadow. "What are you accusing me of?" I asked slowly.

"I'm not accusing you of anything," he said wearily. "You're just being exactly what you are—a winner. Not to mention the living legend of the local sports world."

"Wait a minute, that's not fair."

"No," he said. "What's not fair is that you're on a team that's won every game it's played, and I'm—forget it." He looked at me, as if from a distance, and his voice became much calmer. "You know, you never even asked how the game went today."

To be honest, I hadn't even thought about football all day. "You had a game today?" I asked shakily.

"Yes, we had a game. Against Manchester. Jeez, Megan, is hockey the only thing you care about? Hockey and matchmaking?"

He turned away from me, put his soda down, and took off through the door that led into the yard. I almost let him stalk off by himself, but I guess it was my stubborn streak that took over. I wasn't about to let things end like that.

Outside, Troy was standing beside one of the lawn chairs, staring out into the night.

A cold wind had come up, and I could feel myself shiver as I said, "Look, I've been to almost every game you played. But today I had to get ready for this party, remember?"

"Kelsey was at the game today," he said. "Obviously, she cares enough about Dave to show up all the time. Every Saturday."

"I told you," I said, trying to control my temper, "I was really busy. I was here making seventy-five grinder sandwiches. Can't you be reasonable?"

Troy looked at me for the first time since I'd come outside. "You could have popped over to the school for a little while," he said. "Mike did. I don't think that would have been asking too much. I thought I could count on you."

"Troy—what happened today at the game?"

He spoke slowly, as if trying to make a child understand. "We almost won. We almost won."

"That's terrific! You ought to feel great about it."

"Oh, please, but just the same I wish you'd been there, Megan. For the first time this year everything started to come together. I wish you'd seen us. But I guess you were just too busy."

"Come on," I pleaded, "let's not get into a fight now."

"No, let's not," he agreed. "It's not your fault that you're a born winner and I'm not."

And then I lost it. "Oh, for crying out loud, self-pity is the last thing you—"

He stood, glaring down at me, even more furious than I was. "Oh, self-pity, is it? Is that under the *S* file? Jeez, Megan, do you have a quote from your Dr. Primrose for everything?"

"Pembroke," I told him through clenched teeth. I was beginning to grow sick of this discussion.

"Pembroke, then. And what does Dr. Pembroke say about winners? Maybe that's what I need—pearls of wisdom from Dr. Pembroke!"

"Troy," I said, trying one last time to avoid the disaster I knew was coming. "Forget Dr. Pembroke. Look, I'm really sorry I didn't get to the game today or have the decency to ask you about it. But now—now what I want more than anything is for you and me to go back into the party and—"

"And you always get what you want, don't you, Megan?"

His voice was so angry, I couldn't even answer him.

"Not this time," he said. "I'm getting out of here."

And that time I didn't even try to follow him. I could hear the Brown Monster starting up, and I knew he was really leaving. I felt cold and sick all over.

Chapter Fifteen

"Be careful what you wish for, because you might end up getting it." I pondered those words the next day as I thumbed through my stacks of psychology clippings, trying to find an answer somewhere among the wrinkled, yellowed pages.

There were no answers for me this time, I was beginning to think. But I kept going over that piece of advice that I'd often heard my mother give, about being careful what you wish for—because you might get it.

I had spent the past summer wishing for something I could do well, and, yes—for fame. I had wanted to be well-known at North High, one way or another. Now, because of field hockey, I had that fame, and I didn't want it—not if it meant I had to lose Troy Fennell.

I plunked down on the rug in my room and scanned dozens of headlines. "Are You Truly Prepared For Success?" *No*, I thought.

"Will You Crack Under The Pressure Of Fame?" *Yes*, I thought.

"Is It Easier To Fail Than To Succeed?" *Definitely*, I decided.

Just looking at those headlines made me feel like crying. I was learning, the hard way, that maybe they were right. Fame was a curse!

Actually, I had to admit that wasn't exactly right. The truth was that I had been enjoying all that newspaper publicity and letting myself believe everything they said. To say I'd been acting self-important would be an understatement.

I kept seeing Troy as he had looked the night before, angry with me for not caring about his football games. That was what it was really about. That and my acting as if all that mattered was what *I* wanted. Not the fact that I was the so-called field hockey sensation of North High.

And now I had the definite feeling that I had lost Troy forever.

"Megan, what *happened* last night?" Beth

seemed to materialize out of nowhere. She was standing in my doorway, looking absolutely radiant.

"Oh, Troy and I had a fight," I said, not sure if I wanted to discuss it.

"I guess you did," she said, sitting down beside me. "Megan, I couldn't believe it when he walked out on the party. Mike couldn't, either."

She was waiting for an explanation, so she could try to help me. That's what best friends are for, of course, but instead I changed the subject.

"Beth, tell me something. You and Mike—you really hit it off, didn't you?"

Her eyes gave me the answer. "I know you can't see it because he's your brother, but Mike is the greatest. He's smart and considerate, and, believe it or not, he turned out to be really romantic, too."

"Mike?" In spite of the way I was feeling, I had to laugh. "You're right. I don't see it. But I'm glad he's showing someone his good side. So admit it, Mike was the one you had a crush on, back at the beginning of school?"

She blushed. "I didn't want to tell you back then because it seemed so hopeless. But, Megan, you pushed us together, didn't you? Confess!"

I didn't answer. I was thinking of Friday when

151

I'd bragged to Troy, "I never give up, and I always get results, I just keep going until I get what I want."

Obnoxious. I had been thoroughly obnoxious. No wonder he had gotten fed up with me!

"I know you helped Mike and me," Beth said gently. "But I have a feeling you don't want my help now. Right?"

I nodded miserably. "I appreciate your coming over here, I really do. But maybe I need to work this out on my own."

"OK," she said. "I won't press you. But if you need me, call."

"Sure," I promised. I watched her leave, grateful that at least *she* wasn't mad at me. Beth and Mike would be all right, I was pretty sure of that.

But me? I had been rude and thoughtless. Football meant a lot to Troy, even if his team was less than victorious. And playing meant a lot to him. He cared about the sport, and he was hurt because I hadn't cared. He'd counted on me, and I hadn't been there for him.

I remembered that night after the movies, when he had said, "Do you suppose that's what real caring is? Just being there for each other? Being more concerned about the other person's troubles than your own?"

I groaned out loud. I certainly had let him down.

I started to cry again. This was at least my ninth fit of crying since the night before when Troy had walked away from the party. I couldn't help it. I cried until there weren't any tears left.

"You look sort of pathetic there, Megan," my brother said. He had been standing in the doorway, watching me silently. He was probably right. I was wearing my old blue pajamas with the mended place in the knee, my hair was still uncombed because I hadn't taken my shower yet, and I was sure my face was streaked with tears.

"What is all this?" he asked, coming into the room. "Your how-to-live-right articles? Gads, you have enough of them!"

He didn't seem to be laughing at me, however.

"I suppose you think I'm nuts, too, huh?" I asked, looking up at him with a rueful grin. "Saving all this stuff—trying to find Help by turning to the *H* file?"

"No, you're not nuts, Megan." He sat down on the floor beside me and looked at me with friendly interest.

"Well, tell Troy that," I blurted out without thinking.

"No, I came to talk to *you*," Mike said firmly. "Beth said you didn't feel like talking, but I figured I wouldn't take no for an answer. You're not the only one in this family who's stubborn."

I looked at him with eyes that were about to overflow with tears again. Suddenly I couldn't keep everything inside me.

"Oh, Mike, I've made such a mess of everything. I've lost Troy. He's furious with me *and* disappointed in me."

"Wait a minute, just wait. I can't help you if I don't know what's happening."

"I know, but—well, Mike—you never like to listen to my troubles."

"You mean we haven't been too close. I know, I plead guilty to that," he said. "I admit I was generally selfish and never cared about your problems."

"That seems to run in the family," I said. I wiped away a few tears and looked straight into my brother's dark eyes. "I can't believe you're saying this."

"Come on. I'm not a total monster! I've always been crazy about you, even if I don't show it very much. And, Megan, you did something for me yesterday that I'm aware of, even if it is supposed to be a secret."

"What?" I challenged him.

"You arranged that whole party just for Beth and me, didn't you? Admit it!"

"Well, it worked," I said.

He smiled. "Of course it worked. As soon as we started dancing, I knew we were really attracted to each other. Always had been, I suppose. But I'm kind of a chump when it comes to romance, in case you didn't notice."

I grinned at him. "Of course I noticed. But don't worry, I think you two will make a great couple. Neither of you will ever get so obnoxious that you'd ruin your relationship forever." I started to cry again.

"Come on, Megan, talk to me. Tell me what happened between you and Troy."

So he sat back on his heels while I told him the story of our argument the night before. I tried to remember everything that Troy had said because it seemed important. It *was* important.

"Is he being unfair, or what?" I finished. "I know I was wrong in forgetting about his game, but he wasn't exactly reasonable, either."

"Hmmm." Mike was deep in thought. "He did sort of go off the deep end, didn't he?"

"I thought so. But now I don't even care! I love him, and I want him to love me—"

"Now wait a minute. I'd guess that he overreacted, but maybe he had reason to. Maybe this has been coming on for a while now. You know, like the straw that broke the camel's back?"

"I'm not sure what you mean."

"Well, you admit you've been bragging a little bit, crowing about your success in hockey, and just getting overconfident about all your abilities in general. Even I noticed it, but it didn't really bother me because I'm not your boyfriend."

"The bragging that I did—you think that's why he really walked out on me?"

"I think he was hurt. About a lot of things. The football team being such a disaster. Everyone making such a big deal over you—everyone, including yourself, Megan. And then it seemed as if you didn't even care about what was important to him."

"And of all the games I could have missed, I skipped the one where they almost won. I never really saw him being good at what he loves."

"Yeah." Mike nodded his head. "Troy is not a petty person, or a bitter one. I guess he just felt that he was always there for you at all of your home games—"

"And he was, too," I said mournfully.

"So you could have been there for him."

"Oh, Mike. How could I have been so stupid and blind? All that bragging—and then missing his game—"

"Chalk it up to inexperience, kiddo. You were OK at sports, but inexperienced in the game of love. We all make mistakes."

I sighed deeply. "But it's too late now. I think he really hates me."

"Oh, Megan. I can't believe that. He's been so crazy about you for weeks that I doubt if he can turn off his feelings that easily."

"Thanks, Mike," I said in a croaky voice.

"Think nuttin' of it," he said, joking. "Anyway, what have I done? Not a darn thing. We've discussed the problem but not the solution."

"I know," I said. "Maybe there is no solution. Except that I have to learn to be more humble, so I don't lose every friend I've ever had."

"That wouldn't hurt," Mike said. "Maybe it would help if you think this way: Your talent is a gift, and not something that you invented. And when you have a gift, you can't take complete credit for it."

I could see exactly what he meant. "Is that how you think about your writing?"

"Yes, but let's not get into that now. Look, Megan, you've got to have a chance to talk this out with Troy—no matter what the outcome. At least you'll have the chance to say you're sorry— You *are* sorry, aren't you?"

"Of course! Are you kidding? I could kill myself for not going to that football game yesterday!"

"All right. Let me think about this." Mike sat there and thought for a short time. Then he snapped his fingers, looking really pleased with himself.

"Got it! I'll arrange everything. I'll go over to Troy's in a little while. You, I hope, will have showered by then and made yourself look presentable?"

"Definitely," I said, comforted by the old bantering.

"Good. I'll talk to him and get him to meet you at—where's a good place? Someplace secluded and a place that has some sort of meaning for you? A sentimental place?"

"Oh, I don't know." I started to get all jittery at the very thought of meeting with Troy. "Maybe—the beach down by Dave's house. But that's a private beach, isn't it?"

Mike looked inspired. "Not in October it isn't. All those resident-only restrictions are lifted after Labor Day. So that's it. You'll wait there—where?"

"By the tree where he first kissed me," I said shyly.

"By the tree it will be." Mike jumped up with great purpose and energy. "Now *I* get a chance to play cupid for *you*."

But I had a horrible thought. "What if Troy won't go to the beach, Mike? What if he's totally through with me?"

"He won't say no to me. He'll go, even if it's

just to clear the air, or break up, or whatever. Sorry—I don't mean to upset you, but we have to face the possibilities, here."

"I know," I whispered sadly.

"But, look, the important thing is that you try. So get your hair shampooed and get dressed—"

"I must really be a mess," I said.

"You are. Get fixed up and get on your bike, and be down at the beach in forty-five minutes. Can you do that?"

"Aye-aye, sir. I'm a speed demon on wheels. I can make that bike fly, if I have to—" I stopped short. "Whoops. There I go again. I was bragging, wasn't I?"

Mike nodded. "You have to be careful, Megan. You have a lot of natural abilities—but don't rub them in. After a while it can rankle."

"Rankle?"

"Look that up in your Pembroke," Mike said, starting for the door.

"Hey, Mike—?"

"Yeah?"

"Speaking of Dr. Pembroke, I always thought you were a terribly selfish First Born Child, but maybe you're not so bad, after all. Maybe you've had a few problems yourself, being the first kid and all—"

He rolled his eyes.

I said, "Well, the first one really does have a

159

lot to prove, what with most parents' high expectations. That could be why you worked so hard at writing. Instead of taking the garbage out!"

"Glad you finally recognized that, Meegles," Mike said. "OK, I'm going to talk to Troy. Remember, forty-five minutes from now."

Chapter Sixteen

Rain seemed to be in the air. Dark clouds scudded across the sky, and the leaves that were left on the trees were being blown around in funny little patterns, turning inside out here and there. It was especially gloomy at the shore of Lake Juniper.

I stood at the top of the beach path, staring down at the choppy, dark blue waters. What a difference from the last time I'd been here! That had been a warm summer night, late in August, the official kickoff party for the football and field hockey teams. Everyone had been light-hearted and hopeful, a bunch of wackos having a great time.

Now I shivered and drew my fall jacket tighter

around me. I chained my bike to a tree and began the steep descent past the hemlocks and ferns. I felt completely alone in the dark, damp world along the shore.

But it would be different when Troy got here. We'd be able to talk about our problem, and maybe I could get him to forgive me. I hoped that we could work it out.

I would promise never again to act conceited in any way—no matter what. I would promise to take an interest in Troy's team and be at every game, just be there for support when he needed me. . . .

I would promise . . . I would promise . . .

My mind wouldn't take me any further. I was scared and nervous, my heart going at a frantic pace. I had so much apologizing to do, and I wondered if I could really convince Troy at all.

Sighing, I walked around on the sandy beach, hearing the distant rumble of thunder. The maple trees along the shore were swaying in the wind. The lake began to look darker and more agitated every minute.

I wished Troy would hurry up and get there. I kept checking my wristwatch. I was right on time. But where was he?

When ten minutes had gone by, I began to suspect the worst. Mike couldn't convince Troy to come and talk to me. It was all over. He didn't even want to see me!

When twenty minutes had gone by, I was positive. Troy was not coming. And the skies were threatening to let loose at any second.

Completely miserable, I trudged back up the path toward my bike. I'd just reached the top when a roll of thunder sounded not too far away. Oh, great. Might as well get hit by lightning now, I thought. Everything else has gone wrong.

I undid the chain lock, jumped on the bike, and pedaled off toward home. All I was aware of was a terrible sense of loss. At that point, I felt about as low as I had ever felt.

The rain started, cold and steady, slicing at my back and neck as I rode my bike along wet, quiet back streets. It all suited the way I felt: dismal.

Mike had tried to settle things for Troy and me, and instead I'd been left alone on the beach. That part really hurt.

I pictured myself being all alone, maybe even for the rest of my life. Somehow—though I couldn't imagine how—I would have to go on living without Troy. Somehow I would have to find a way to pick up the pieces of Megan Carter and glue them back together again.

For starters, I was thinking, I'd do things with Jessica. She and I had never been terribly close, but once hockey season was over, I'd have some time to spend with her. We could take the bus to the mall and go Christmas shopping together. We could have long talks and lots of silly, giggling times. We could share a lot more than nail polish and barrettes. We could become real sisters, for the first time.

Thinking that way helped a little bit. And so, looking and feeling like a drowned rat, I turned down my street.

Someone was out on our front lawn, standing under the giant weeping willow. Probably Mike, I thought, waiting to tell me that Troy was through with me.

But it wasn't Mike. The tall figure under the tree, as wet and sodden as I was, began to look more and more like Troy as I drew closer. But— what on earth would Troy be doing there?

I got off the bike and approached the tree cautiously, one hand holding the handlebars and the other brushing back rain and hair from my face.

"Megan?" I heard him say. "Oh, I'm so glad I finally found you—"

He came rushing toward me, and I put the bike gently down on the grass. He had rain streaming through his hair and down his face, but he had never looked better to me.

"I don't understand," I said, trying to talk through the downpour. "What are you doing here?"

"I came looking for you more than an hour ago. Your parents and Jessica didn't know where you'd gone. So I decided to wait right here until you got back from wherever you went."

"But you were supposed to meet me at the beach."

"Beach?" He looked genuinely puzzled. "What beach? What are you talking about? Did we have a date at the beach?"

I scanned his face. "Didn't Mike talk to you?"

"No."

"I guess you weren't home when he went to your house. You were on your way over here, instead."

"I suppose so. Why was Mike going to my house?"

"Oh, so you and I could meet, and try to talk. I waited at the beach for such a long time—and I was positive I'd never see you again, but—"

He was silent for a while.

"I came to apologize, Megan."

Stunned, I put my hand to my mouth. "No, don't say that. I'm the one who has to apologize."

"No way." His voice sounded grim and regretful. "I behaved like a spoiled little kid last night, and I ruined your party for you. And I am so sorry, Megan. For all of it."

"Troy, that's crazy. I was the horrible one! Always talking about my hockey games, and never caring about football—"

"Just that once, Megan. Come on, you went to other football games this year. You only missed one, and I went and made a federal case out of it."

"This is weird," I said in a low voice. "Do you want to go into the house? It's pouring. . . ."

"No," Troy said. "It's not bad under the tree, and it's much more private." We moved under the spreading shelter of the big old willow, dragging my bike in with us.

"I can't believe this," I said. "You were coming here to apologize, and I was doing the same thing, rushing off to meet you at the beach to say I'm sorry. . . ."

"Great minds think alike," he quipped, but his brown eyes looked deadly serious. He put out his arms, and I moved slowly into them. They were warm and strong and so comforting.

"I'll never do it again," we both said at the exact same time. Then we looked at each other and burst out laughing.

Troy brushed a strand of wet hair out of my eyes. "I thought I'd lost you," he said softly.

I shook my head.

"I know," he said. "You never give up."

"It's not that," I said. "It's just that I couldn't give up someone who means so much to me."

He tilted my chin up to look into my eyes, and for once I didn't look away. Somehow I wasn't afraid to say it now. "You know, I think I may have loved you since Winchester Pond. It just took me awhile to realize it."

"Not me." His eyes held me, warm and steady. "I've always known."

I stood on tiptoe to plant a kiss along the curve of his cheek. His skin felt wonderful, slightly stubbly and totally wet. He folded me into his arms, and I could feel my heart dancing inside my chest.

We stood like that for a while, under the willow tree, with the rain streaming down around us. Then before I knew it our mouths came together, so that we stood kissing under the tree, right on my front lawn. And who cared if any of the neighbors saw us?

Sometimes nothing else matters but a kiss, at the right time and with the right boy.

That was one of those times, one that would stay with me forever.

We hope you enjoyed reading this book. If you would like to receive further information about titles available in the Bantam series, just write to the address below, with your name and address:

Kim Prior
Bantam Books
61–63 Uxbridge Road
Ealing
London W5 5SA

If you live in Australia or New Zealand and would like more information about the series, please write to:

Sally Porter
Transworld Publishers (Aust.) Pty. Ltd.
15–23 Helles Avenue
Moorebank
N.S.W. 2170
AUSTRALIA

Kiri Martin
Transworld Publishers (N.Z.) Ltd.
Cnr. Moselle and Waipareira Avenues
Henderson
Auckland
NEW ZEALAND

All Bantam Young Adult books are available at your bookshop or newsagent, or can be ordered from the following address:

Corgi/Bantam Books
Cash Sales Department
PO Box 11
Falmouth
Cornwall
TR10 9EN

Please list the title(s) you would like, and send together with a cheque or postal order. You should allow for the cost of the book(s) plus postage and packing charges as follows:

All orders up to a total of £5.00   50p
All orders in excess of £5.00   Free

Please note that payment must be made in pounds sterling; other currencies are unacceptable.

(The above applies to readers in the UK and Republic of Ireland only)

B.F.P.O. customers, please allow for the cost of the book(s) plus the following for postage and packing: 60p for the first book, 25p for the second book and 15p per copy for the next 7 books, thereafter 9p per book.

Overseas customers, please allow £1.25 for postage and packing for the first book, 75p for the second book, and 28p for each subsequent title ordered.

Thank you!

Janet Quin-Harkin's
Sugar & Spice

Watch out for a smashing new series from the best-selling author, Janet Quin-Harkin.

Meet the most unlikely pair of best friends since Toni and Jill from Janet Quin-Harkin's TEN BOY SUMMER.

Caroline's thrilled to find out she's got a long-lost cousin exactly her age. But she's horrified when Chrissy comes to spend a year with her family. Caroline's a reserved and polite only child – now she has to share her life with a loud, unsophisticated, embarrassing farm girl!

Coming soon – wherever Bantam paperbacks are sold!

Other series from Bantam Books for Young Readers
Ask your bookseller for the books you have missed